All Men Are Strangers

Also by Lauran Paine
in Large Print:

The Long Years

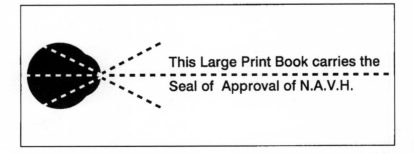

This Large Print Book carries the
Seal of Approval of N.A.V.H.

All Men Are Strangers

Lauran Paine

Thorndike Press • Waterville, Maine

Published in 2002 by arrangement with
Golden West Literary Agency.

Thorndike Press Large Print Paperback Series.

The tree indicium is a trademark of Thorndike Press.

The text of this Large Print edition is unabridged.
Other aspects of the book may vary from the original edition.

Set in 16 pt. Plantin by Myrna S. Raven.

Printed in the United States on permanent paper.

Library of Congress Cataloging-in-Publication Data

Paine, Lauran.
    All men are strangers / Lauran Paine.
      p. cm.
    ISBN 0-7862-4149-7 (lg. print : sc : alk. paper)
    1. Large type books.   I. Title.
    PS3566.A34 A45 2002
    813'.54—dc21   2002019964

All Men Are Strangers

Chapter One

They saw him as a stranger to the little town Malta; this grey, gaunt man in his middle thirties with intense eyes, a mouth that was bitter and an invulnerable strength to him. He strode through the town, his spurs ringing, with a long, springing stride as though in a hurry to meet destiny head on. His jaw was thrust forward, his big gun riding at his hip and the long brown tails of his dust-coloured coat swinging out behind.

He had a subtlety that was quickness and no shred of fear. He would stand wide-legged against ten and shoot with a cold laughter lying deep in his hazel eyes. He could ride like the wind and fade into the night like a wraith. He could be tender with a horse and favouring to a dying enemy, yet in the town of Malta they saw him for nearly what he was — never guessing the rest of it even though the brimstone scent of trouble ran in his wake.

Three months before he had served with the U.S. Dragoons along the Utah line and when Brigham Young laid aside his bombast in the face of Johnston's Army and bowed to power greater than his, the volunteers had been mustered out. He had bought new clothes and struck out for The Nations and home — this quiet man with the aura of power to him.

And home had shown him a letter from Malta '. . . they make it hard, Jack, but a man's to fight if he's to hold his own.'

And a second letter came later. '. . . by persons unknown. We give him a decent burial at the Malta graveyard . . .'

He had walked out into the spring with the terrible evil eating his heart out. Then he saddled up and rode overland to the cowtown of Malta in the Territory of Arizona. He came to see the lifting, running country as his brother had seen it. A great wilderness where sweat would soften the earth toward men. He liked it — and he hated it, and he said nothing to anyone but to the sheriff who had written that second letter.

Sheriff Amos Marlow was almost as tall, almost as gaunt and brimstone-like as he was, but much older. Older in mind and body, but more still, he had an oldness of spirit that came from constant disillusionment. The hope had all ebbed away.

"Will Fulton's brother? Well, there's little I can tell, Fulton. Will kept to hisself pretty much. He give no trouble and he asked for none." Amos struggled with words. They had never been easy to him, nor kind either, and in times like this they almost failed him altogether.

"Will come like a lot of 'em come, Fulton. Full of hope and grit."

"I knew my brother," the hazel-eyed stranger said. "There's nothing you need tell me about him — except who shot him."

"That I don't know."

"I can see you wouldn't," the stranger said evenly. "I can see you wouldn't." He got up and hooked his thumb inside his dun-coloured coat and gazed broodingly down at Amos Marlow. "I'll find out who did it. I'll find out why they did it, too."

Amos was patient with men deep in grief. There was a warped kind of gentleness to him that a few dying men had seen and taken away with them; few others even suspected it for it didn't show in the cragginess of his features nor in the level impassiveness of his eyes. "Don't set yourself against the law, Fulton," Amos said slowly. "It'll come out one day, then the law'll take care of whoever done it."

The gaunt stranger's brooding glance hung. "I can't wait," he said, and left Amos Marlow's office.

He went out to the Malta graveyard in the

late night when the spring winds were worrying at the eaves of the town and men were either in saloons or in bed. There he knelt in the mud where the rain had washed brown streaks in the sere old face of the earth. He thought; *Dead at thirty when his sap was running the fullest. God, I have asked you for little. Let me serve you in this vengeance which is yours.*

With the coming of daylight the stranger was riding his big ugly horse north out of Malta. He rode as far as the soddy, with the failing little peach trees planted close by it, a hut set low and snug against the earth in this wide land that was lonely without life in it. Will's homestead in the Arizona country was a vast roll, spreading in rise and fall and hushed beauty until it merged with the sky. The spring was firm now, and the wild geese going by far overhead, northward, cried mournfully down to the big stranger on the ugly horse. The warm air from Mexico was full and strong with new life and his brother wasn't there to sniff it.

He got down and felt the vacantness of the place. Moving, a long way off, were some antelope. Closer, there was a scolding of prairie chickens in the sage and new grass.

A little lost wind made the sagging door

protest. Here was the worst kind of loneliness: the kind death leaves behind.

He walked with his big springing stride to the soddy, ducked 'way low and pushed inside where the mildew smell came quickly to engulf him. In the dimness he found a candle and lit it and held it high. Nothing but wreckage. A broken little table, three stools and a lovingly made willow rocker that was harbouring a wood-rat's nest now. Small, frightened sounds of things.

Outside he went into the simple horse shed. There were old droppings there and a cribbed manger where a horse had fretted. Some whittled pegs were set deep into a squared upright where a saddle had hung. Cow sign too, but faint with the drift of winter's wash.

There was a partially finished, sagging henhouse. He looked in there and found feathers where a skunk had held forth in rich living until the last hen was eaten.

Nothing . . .

He sat down in the sunny south of the cabin and made a cigarette and thought of Will. The flash of Will's eyes in anger and their outpouring of pleasure. The way his head rode full and proud on his neck. The breadth of his shoulders and the trust in him, like a woven fibre that made up his

11

weal. And of Will's quickness, like his own, with a carbine and a Colt. As he sat there smoking, unmindful of the world, thinking, his eyes pale and cold like tawny agates in ice water, ringed with darkness beneath them, he wondered what there was in Will's life that had prompted a man to shoot him in the back from hiding and leave him for the coyotes to worry with their small, sharp teeth.

Of all his family of men — his silent father and four huge brothers — Will had taken the greatest portion of his love, for Will was unlike the others. He was somehow the strangest of the lot, for he laughed. He threw his head far back so that the sun shone off his stiff blond hair, and he laughed. Not many Fulton men ever did that, but Will had.

And Will had loved life; he trusted it and accepted it. He wore his trust outward, like a flag. It was in his open face and his sparkling eyes. Who would kill a man like Will, and why?

He got up and ground the cigarette in his big fist. Looking down at the door stoop in spite of himself, he saw the dark-splashed stains there. He let the broken body of the cigarette fall from his hand and went back to the horse, mounted and reined farther out into the land that was his dead brother's. He rode for hours, guessing where the boundary lines would be, but there was nothing anywhere to indicate a purpose for murder, he hadn't really expected to find one, so he reined toward the town again and cutting across the north-south stage road, swung down it.

A loping cowboy came pelting through the heat behind him. When they were abreast the rider reined up with an open smile. "Howdy; spring's here an' a man comes alive again."

"Howdy."

"You fer Malta too?" The man's eyes shone with the flow of his blood, much as a rutting buck's eyes would shine.

"Yes."

"M'name's Joe Halter — hell of a name f'a man rides horses, ain't it." The laughter pealed richly into the sparkling sunlight.

The big, gaunt stranger said nothing nor looked around at the rider. A terrible awkwardness settled swiftly. The rider looked stunned. He gazed at the flinty profile. The warmth died slowly from his face, like a summer twilight dying stubbornly, then without a word he spurred his horse and loped on down the stage road toward town. The stranger's hazel glance followed him with a solemnity that was solid.

Amos Marlow saw him enter the Cash House Café from the opposite side of the road where he was leaning on an overhang upright. He shifted his tobacco and spat thoughtfully. *Fulton; Will Fulton's brother. Hmph! Plumb forgot t'ask him his first handle. It doesn't matter. Don't it? Man can't never be certain. Not with those gloomy silent ones.*

He stepped down off the plankwalk and crossed through the springy softness of the drying roadway, heading for the café. You couldn't tell a damned thing about those real quiet, secretive ones, ever. Some of the biggest bluffs on earth, and some of the biggest cyclones too. One thing certain — they were the biggest.

Fulton ordered fried strips of beef and eggs. His eyes had a sort of racked vacancy while he ate. When the sheriff came in and dropped down beside him he didn't look up. The coffee was strong enough to float a horseshoe.

"You been out to his claim?"

The hazel eyes moved up and around slowly. "Yes."

"Find anything?"

"No."

"I didn't either." Marlow nodded at the watery-eyed oldster who ran the café.

"Coffee, Eb. Nothin' t'eat; just coffee." To the other, "I forgot to ask your first handle, Fulton."

The gaunt man was eating again. He answered brusquely without glancing up. "Jack," he said, then, "Did my brother rub some cowman the wrong way?"

Amos shook his head and blew into the syrupy coffee. "Naw. They don't pay much attention to squatters out here. Will was a pleasant cuss anyway." He sighed and sipped his coffee with a quick puckering of his forehead. "It don't fit any idea I can figure, Fulton."

"I heard this was rich land out here," Jack Fulton said bitterly. "Will's trees are dyin' out there."

"You got to have water in this country if you got nothing else."

"Didn't Will have water?"

"I don't know. Didn't look the place over like that. I just wanted some tracks — something like that." Marlow put aside the acid tasting coffee and fished for his tobacco sack. "One thing about this country, Fulton, it's hard. You got to stand hardness and stand to give as hard as you get."

Fulton finished eating and pushed the plate aside. He spoke without looking around at Amos Marlow. "I can do that,

15

sheriff. I can give as hard as I get." He said it grimly, then he pushed upright, dropped some silver coins on the plank counter and strode back out where the scent of spring was rich and pleasant and the sun was out with a vengeance.

He made a cigarette, standing a little apart from the ebb and flow of humanity. The smoke added a little to the general fragrance of the spring air. The land of Arizona was running full with the strong, warm sap of new life. Deep within Jack Fulton stirred the age-old urge of men who are close to the earth. To sow, to reap, to put their hands to the soil. It was spring, 1884.

He threw aside the cigarette and drew in a deep, strong breath. He was busy with some seed in his mind for a long time, then he went across the road to the livery-barn, hired a wagon and a team, drove them to Murphy's Emporium and bought supplies. Amos Marlow watched him load up with a hooded look. His face had the inscrutability of a knowing man fingering, lightly, speculations that weren't surprising.

Jack drove the wagon all the way to Will's claim. He worked until the sweat ran off him in trickles and it took him two days to set the cabin to rights, find the spring, return the wagon and fetch back his big ugly horse. It was labour with a purpose and afterward, established in dead Will's place, he scoured the land again. There was nothing.

The days dragged.

He planted a garden and stolidly toted water from the well to it. He even rented a team and sowed a hay crop of oats. The claim thrived under his hand, but he never was out of reach of his carbine. Working close, it leaned against a stone row or a tree trunk or lay across his lap. His pistol was with him too and his hard hazel eyes, never quiet, searching the brooding land for an enemy, were like the eyes of an Indian; restless, wild looking with a tawniness to them, deadly and eager to kill first.

Two days of drizzling, gloomy rain came and assured Jack of his hay crop. He rode out in it the second day when he knew from the clouds the wet was soon to pass. Riding in a great circle, leaving his tracks for the world to see, he made a circuit of Will's claim deliberately, his tall frame upright and dark with glistening water and his flat mouth flatter, the hazel eyes gleaming with a depth of fierceness. Very purposefully he exposed himself and his doings to the land, and a cold-running coiledness lay in him waiting to strike.

The day after the rain the warmth came

again. There were birds and steam from the wrung-out earth and new grass flourished until the land of Arizona in the late spring was an emerald carpet stretching out into eternity. The afternoon moved in and the sun went lower throwing a hard lemon glitter over the earth. Jack smoked with his back to the horse shed watching Arizona — waiting, waiting.

Back home in The Nations men rode often in the night. Indian and white and sometimes — but not often — together. It wasn't a rare thing to find a man shot through the heart in his field. There was the trouble men were born to, back there. The Nations — a land where the herded Indians were driven like cattle, corraled within unseen lines on a bleak, dusty earth, and left to work out a destiny no one was certain about.

Jack's father had harshly told his four sons one time: "Ideas? Give 'em up. If ye want to live ye've got t'fight. Ye'll need to be a man or ye'll get plowed under. Don't hope fer happiness here. Who are ye t'hope fer it here? There's n'happiness fer ye now, an' I don't reckon there ever will be. Be hard, be quick an' strong. Shoot first and look second. I raised ye believin' as I say now and n'man can stand aga'n ye. Redskin or Whiteskins — ye've been raised to match 'em and send 'em t'hell an' chase 'em fer two days over the coals. And remember this — ye're a family, and s'long as ye stand fer one 'nother ye'll never fail. But let one o' ye peel off and ye'll need more'n God or me ta he'p ye!"

Fulton sat there with his cold glance sweeping the land — waiting — thinking of the old man and the others. Of them all, only young Will had dared to laugh and walk alone, seeking what he had told Jack there was in the world: goodness, laughter, a wealth of wonderful things that weren't in Oklahoma — The Nations. Will meant to find them. Jack spat, cleared his throat and spat again. Will had found them all right — a goddamned .45-.70 slug that broke his spine and blew most of his lungs and soft parts out through his shirt front.

He got up with the humid heat beating against his body like little invisible fists. He held his carbine loosely, like a man might who had a familiarity and a thorough knowledge and easy acceptance that guns were like britches — you didn't go without them.

He watched Arizona turn soft and mellow in the warm evening and smiled a little at it. Arizona was new. He came from an older land where the blood-currents were swifter, bleaker, more savage and hurting. He was here with his long training. Arizona had its Apaches, its badmen. It swaggered and talked hard — but it didn't have the deep ruthlessness, the long training in fierceness that a man from an older, hardened, established land had. He was here to teach Arizona.

He waited until the darkness was fully upon the land before he moved back to the soddy. Inside he leaned the carbine close to the door and set the rocker Will had made of creek willows by the window. Lighting the coal-oil lantern, he hung it from its square nail overhead and went back outside again.

There were more frogs tonight. They made a languid, rasping sound as though the heat rising out of the swampy land made them drowsy. Some coyotes a long way off sounded to the moon that was doubled over as if it were in pain. A low-flying owl went skimming earthward, eerie big eyes, like dun-yellow marbles, seeking kangaroo rats and feeding mice.

Jack looked like a tall image carved to represent The Listener. He had a tight piece of sacking pulled down over his carbine so that only the trigger and trigger-guard showed in the watery light. He might have been a statue made of dull, dusty old stone, until you saw his eyes — eyes with something eagle-like showing, and something hurting, too. The iron jut of his jaw and the wide mouth were drawn in bitterness.

He went out a ways as he had done every night. There was an unknown force of evil in this land, and yet it was in him to like Arizona despite its immaturity and its fierce foolishness. The plains were wide, swept now by the wrath of men with lawlessness running them. Plains that at this moment stretched free beneath the light of the ill moon and the lanterns in the night, the stars. It was a beautiful land. A godless plain of evil and murder and lawlessness, but he was used to such places.

At home it had been far, far worse. There was no justice in either place except the justice a man carried strongly in his hand and wore girded to his middle. Nor was there peace and Jack Fulton, like all the Fultons except young Will, was steeped in a way of life founded on these things. It was this environment he moved in now, stalking softly, his grey, gaunt frame blending, moving through the poignant fragrance of a late spring night with his long stride and his covered gun and his deep-brooding patience greater than any Indian had — waiting.

He had no wildness in him such as an Indian would have had. Only a natural fierceness that lay sheathed and dormant, slumbering, waiting. A deadliness that found repose in the long black hours. A strange serenity of resolve in a spirit made dark and willing and infinitely patient.

At length he heard that which was his long reward. The fruitfulness of all he had done, coming to pass. Horses, rein-chains and rubbing leather: movement in the night . . .

He was like a knurl of the night, a part of it, his head up as though to sniff the strangeness that was out there, east of the sod house. Only the faintest tingling ran along his nerves. Just a small quivering of the nostrils showed that he had heard at all. Then he lifted the carbine, cocked it and held it lightly, waiting.

Minutes were chained and dragging. Time was lost somewhere east of him. The sounds were gone but the vibrations in the air remained. He felt them, waiting.

Down in the soddy the lantern burned with a yellow-orange intensity as though snarling at the gloom of the night. Light spilled out past the rocker, limning the thing, casting a long, willow shadow onto the dusty earth. He waited . . .

The single shot shattered the night with echoes that ran outward, flinging themselves against the hush like blows from a huge and invisible hammer. Jack raised his carbine, held it aloft for a still second and laid back against the trigger.

The second shot was even more startling. A quickening shimmer of shock was in the atmosphere. He didn't lever in another bullet until he was moving obliquely away from where he had been waiting, and then he did it smoothly like a man who had years of practice behind him. Smoothly, without desperation or slamming, the bullet slid into the short gun's mechanism.

He walked in a large circle around the back of the soddy and stopped, poised, listening. Now there was an even deeper silence to the night than there had been before. A stillness made up of the tensed hush of night animals frozen into immobility. He heard horses moving swiftly a long way off. He looked eastward into the brooding darkness. There was nothing to see, but the distant sounds came back softly.

He went where his blanket was and squatted like an Indian, sure there was no longer a need for vigilance, but awake and wary all the same. The night moved on then, as though time were hastening to catch up with its destiny after having stopped for those brief moments of gunfire. He was still hunkered with the old blanket around his shoulders and the covered carbine athwart his lap, when the greyness of dawn came.

The hours passed. Gloom hung heavy over the ranch yard. Jack had no strained restlessness in him, only a vague, grim depth of satisfaction. When it was light enough to see good, he made a long careful study of the land. If the strangers had left an assassin behind he couldn't find him, and he had studied that land very well, so well, in fact, that he knew he was alone. Days of mentally marking the land, the thickets, even the shadows and places where a man might hide, rewarded his patience now. There was no one waiting for him, he was certain.

Arising, he took the blanket and walked down to the front of the soddy.

The body there was sprawled, stiffening. The carbine lay with its snout buried in the warming earth where a thin layer of dust had flung itself over the weapon. The man — when Jack rolled him over with his gunbarrel — was young and dry-eyed. He had a stingy fuzz of blond whiskerstubble. He was thickly made, powerful of shoulder and short of arm. His faded britches were tucked into high cowhide boots with drover's heels. They were flat, run-over and scuffed looking. The man had walked, when he walked at all, where there were rocks and flinty soil.

The bullet had struck him under the arm on the left side and traversed the width of his lung-cage. He had died almost instantly.

Kneeling, the hazel of his glance deeper, almost brown, Jack drew out the man's wallet and rifled it. There was a wad of old, weary, sweat-limp bills in it and a letter addressed to Colt Burrows, Malta, Arizona Territory. It was from a girl up in Utah. It was a sly kind of a letter with double meanings shot through it. Jack read it with a twisted feeling of contempt and shoved it back into Burrows' wallet.

He got up looking at the dead man thoughtfully. He turned and followed the line of sight of Burrows. The rocking chair was still visible, but awry now, swung away from the window a little. The lantern was burning feebly. He crossed to the soddy, ducked low and went in. The rope-wrapped bundle sitting in the chair, that had been wearing his hat, was sprawled with tufts of torn cloth showing where the bullet had struck.

He very deliberately stoked up a fire, made a fried breakfast and ate standing up. Then he went out to the horse shed, saddled his big horse and led it to the dead man.

There was just enough stiffness to make handling the body easy. He tied him crossways and mounted too. His carbine was bare now, the sacking coverlet left behind as he struck out through the morning sun-splash toward Malta.

It got hot, the sun was on him. He was without cover except for his hat. The ugly big horse raised a heavy kind of yellow-grey dust. He grew thirsty before he came in sight of the village and impatient as well. The sun was smashing at the earth, laying a sullen glow over the thriving new grass and bursting buds. It hurt his eyes a little because they were blood-shot with lack of sleep and grating in their sockets.

When he came close to the tame lands where Malta lay in its majestic setting — a liver-spot on the great belly of the lifting, settling land — he passed people. Some in tired old wagons, others in buggies, more a-horseback. He recognised none of them nor more than looked at them. In Malta it was the same. He went down the dusty roadway with his grisly burden and didn't draw rein until he was before Marlow's office.

There he tied up, stalked across the roadway, up onto the plankwalk and pushed back the sheriff's office door. He closed it partly, gently, behind him. The sheriff had arrived not long before. He still wore his droopy old hat, with its dust-caked sweat streaks and its shapelessness, that was more aged than forlorn. He looked at Jack Fulton a full five seconds, seeing his face, his deep-lying satisfaction, and his tiredness.

"I got a man outside, sheriff."

"Yeah. Who is he?"

"He's dead."

Marlow didn't spring erect. If anything he sagged a little, looking resigned and bone-weary. He moved toward the door without speaking, shouldered past Jack Fulton and went outside. There were other people out there already — men and boys. They were standing in simulated indifference, so palpably false it reeked in a silent, stony way. Amos Marlow went around the horse's rump, lifted the head, stared into the face and let it drop. His breath rattled out of him. He shot a glance at the bystanders, all watching him with silent interest. "Lewt, how about you an' John taking him off the horse an' down to the doctor's shed?"

While the two men moved forward, shufflingly, avoiding the tall, grey frame of Jack Fulton, Amos turned with a despairing glance and rolled his head toward the office. "Come on in, Fulton."

Jack followed him back inside. He felt the

wet eyes following him. He closed the door tightly and stood wide-legged, his hand hooked inside his old dun-coloured coat in a habitual gesture. The hazel eyes, ringed with a deeper purple now, were patient. "Well," he said.

"Sit down." Marlow sat with a little sigh. The gaunt man made no move to comply. "Fulton, did you go through his pockets?"

"Yes, his name's Colt Burrows."

"I know his name," Amos said slowly. "I know his paw's name too, and his sister's name. Does it mean anything to you, his name?"

"Nothing."

Marlow's resignedly thoughtful look held to Jack's face. "No? Well — it might. How'd you come to shoot him?"

"Like I told you. I couldn't wait for you to find Will's murderer. I figured whoever he was didn't kill Will over some silly thing like a woman or a horse. The claim was tied in, some way. I moved out there, put in a crop, planted a garden — did all the things a man'd do who figured on staying."

"All right," Sheriff Marlow said. "I understand that part of it. I figured you were doing it like that. I been watching you come and go. What I want to know is just how you shot him?"

"I made a dummy and left it in Will's rocker by the window. Every night I went outside where I could watch the soddy."

"Oh, you slept out."

"I didn't sleep. I did that when I could, during the day. I figured the bushwhacker'd come back as soon as he saw the place was lived in again. He did. He came last night. There was more'n one of them. Three, I think, judging by the horse-sounds afterward. I watched him come down by the house. After he shot at my dummy in the rocker, I shot him."

"Like that," Amos Marlow said dryly, looking at the tall man's granite face.

"Just like that," Fulton threw back at him.

Marlow motioned toward a chair and leaned on his desk. "There'll be a hearin', of course. Probably won't amount to much. You killed him. He isn't shot in the back. He's dead and you're alive." Marlow shrugged. "Your word's all they'll have."

"It's good enough," Jack said flatly.

"Is it?" the sheriff said, casting a sidling, thoughtful glance his way. "I wonder. You're a stranger in Malta."

"He was stalking me."

"Maybe that's true too, I can't say." Amos leaned far back in his chair gazing up at Jack. "It's natural for folks to be suspicious of strangers. Not just in Malta, but every-where. I reckon was I to do what you've done, in your home town, Fulton, folks'd be suspicious o' me. Whatever I did next, whether it had any bearin' on the killing or not, might influence 'em enough so's they might hang me when my hearin' came up."

Fulton's dark eyes shone with a sardonic intensity. "Are you warning me against the people around here?" he asked.

Marlow shook his head slowly back and forth. "No, I'm not in a position to warn you. I'm the law. I'm just tellin' you how folks are. I've lived a lot longer'n you have. I know those things from experience." Marlow's faded gaze hung saturninely on Fulton's features. "Sit down, and I'll tell you who that was you shot." He let it lie there between them, waiting. In this small way he had the whip-hand. He knew it and Jack knew it. It was one of Marlow's oldest ruses. It had served him well to gain an insight into how a man worked, whether he complied or not. Jack Fulton didn't comply. He showed a wooden little grin around his big mouth and shook his head negatively.

"I know who he was. Colt Burrows. It means nothing to me."

"Yes it does," Marlow said incisively. "It may not now but it will shortly." He knew

Fulton wasn't going to sit down. He had one answer to the man's character. You might drag him to death behind a wild horse, but you'd never trick him or compromise him into doing anything he didn't want to do. That kind of a man.

Marlow had been afraid of that. Now, he sat there gripping the arms of his old chair, worrying. There was trouble coming, sure as God made green grass, there was trouble coming.

"Colt Burrows is the youngest son of Abe Burrows. Abe has another son and a daughter. The boy's name is Mark. The girl's name is Suzanne. Abe's like rawhide and buffalo gut. Mark's — well — he's one to watch, that's all I'm going to say about him." Marlow's gaze became sardonic again. "Now do you see what I've been driven' at? You killed Colt. He was the pet o' the tribe. Now then, they'll be after your guts and no mistake about it neither. The thing is, before your hearin' over the shootin' of Colt comes up, folks hereabouts'll be watching you. Make a wrong play, Fulton, and what the Burrows' don't do, a coroner's jury might do for 'em."

"I'll take the chance," Jack said evenly. "You might pass it on to these Burrowses that if they want me I'll be to home, and if they come onto that claim I'll kill 'em — if I can."

"Whoa," Amos Marlow said quickly. "Slow up. If a little friendly advice don't mean anything to you and you're hell bent on war, then I'll make it stronger. There'll be no feudin' around here. The next time you get in trouble, Fulton, I'll lock you up."

"I'm after no trouble, sheriff. I wanted a murderer and I think I've got him. Why he did it, I don't know. That's the next thing on my list. When I find that out I'll be through here. Until I find it out, I'm stayin', and if seein' me around makes the dead man's kinsmen itch to try their guns, I can't help it. If you want peace, just pass it along what I said. If they don't bother me I won't bother them. That's how it stands. Is that fair or isn't it?"

"That's not the point," the sheriff said sharply. "What counts here is how you behave. We don't want no fighting. You remember that, boy."

Jack's eyes shone with a silky scorn. "I told you I'm not looking for trouble, but if it comes, you'll find me right handy at carin' for myself."

Amos Marlow shoved up out of his chair. "You got your warning. I'll be around to see how you act. Now, let's go over to the judge's office and make out the papers that'll set a date for your hearing."

The judge was a short, plump, perspiring man. He accepted what he had already heard about with aplomb. Only a little curiosity showed in his face, when he sized up Jack Fulton. He didn't say twenty words, all told. The hearing was set for July, two months off, and Sheriff Marlow walked back out into the dazzling light with Jack. On the scuffed plankwalk he stopped and teetered on his boot heels. "The best thing you could do, Fulton, is saddle up and ride. Keep out of the country until your hearin', then come back and get it over with."

Jack nodded down at him with a stony, blank look, said nothing and struck out across the dust and traffic of the roadway for his horse. He rode north out of Malta with a host of eyes following him. Immunity to things like that gave him an aloofness.

He rode steadily toward the soddy, then swung off the trail abruptly and made for a wild timbered part of the country far beyond Will's claim. The day deepened with him threading his way through this darkened and gloomy country. He had wondered about it before but had never ridden out long enough to explore it. Now he did.

There were dark rocks jutting from the

ancient soil and a smell of beauty and patience in the fir-scented air. He sat on a frowning out-thrust and looked into the broad valley below where a little creek meandered. Under the trees was a soft silence and agelessness that let no sunshine through. The heat was far less, too.

He dismounted and made a cigarette and hunkered, for below him was the first habitation he'd seen beyond the soddy. The place had a drenching of shade over it softening the crudeness of the squat cabin. There was a grey barn weathered and listing. A corral of saplings held horses. A few old cows, unafraid, hung around a laboriously made widened place by the creek where watercress grew in strangling profusion.

The scene was one of peace and timelessness. But also, Jack got the impression of vacantness. Nothing moved. It was as though people had left the ranch without a backward glance. A shivering tension was in the air along with the vacantness.

Smoking his cigarette to death, he crushed it out and continued to study the place. Not until a little freshet of limping wind came hurrying through the trees did he get up and guess that it was nearing evening. Then he mounted and wheeled back toward the twisting, panting trail that had led him up there, and rode down toward the soddy.

The early evening was strange too, for the time of the year. It held his attention almost as much as the land he rode over, for there was an ashen gloom to it. A sharp little wind was blowing from the south in a fitful, erratic way. The sky was dense with a thickness of boding to it and mists came scudding before the low ground-wind.

He rode within a mile of Will's soddy and sought a place among some scrub-oaks to make a dry camp. Environmental training ordered it so, for if the Burrows were going to strike in their raging agony they would do it quickly. By now they surely knew Colt was dead, if they hadn't guessed it the night before.

He dismounted and loosened the cincha on his big horse. Slipping off the bridle, he fashioned running-hobbles out of one split rein, took down his carbine and left the animal. Swinging with his big stride over the tall, soft grass, he went down toward the dark gloominess that was the soddy. His old blanket he dragged where some wiry sage would background him, and there he made ready for the long wait. There was another whole night to go through.

35

He was very still. It was a leashed stillness. The real feeling in him was visible only in his eyes. His hands were like stone, steady and relaxed around the carbine in his lap. His darkness of spirit with its incredible patience was ice over ferment — a leashed fierceness.

, He waited he knew not for what, but he never questioned the wisdom of waiting. He never had, not since the first buck he had stalked, and waited for with all the timelessness of an Indian. Even his brothers, who had also been trained in this vast way of rewarding patience, were awed by the endlessness Jack had in him for waiting; for never moving, never drowsing, barely breathing, only his hazel eyes, austere, shifting fluidly, seeing things, piercing the night like the yellow eyes of an owl, tawny, waiting, deadly beyond reckoning. He heard the night around him and felt it; was, in fact, a part of it.

So the strange little wind went hurrying in erratic starts and stops and the shadows turned to gloom. Jack sat there in his old blanket, waiting out the night long hours. It was a small price to pay for life. He had no illusions. Maybe they wouldn't come this soon but he had no way of knowing, so he took the cautious way.

The soddy was forlorn, a dimly seen shape with a darkness to it that was ghostly. A dark squareness against a lighter darkness that was the wind-whipped night. The moon, fuller by scant inches, and the lanterns that hung tiny and resplendent around it, were glistening there, but they offered little to the watching man. It wasn't until just before dawn when the wind hushed quickly and the night seemed to hold its breath, waiting too, and the stillness came tiptoeing with fabulous stealth, that Jack understood what lay ahead. He swore to himself in a low, firm voice.

Then the rain came.

Not in droplets and straight-down benevolence, but in a wildly driven, slanting fury that scourged the land. Beat upon it with clenched, elfin fists made stinging-hard with a drenching intensity. Jack looked at the sky. There were a few stars yet showing. There was small consolation in that for the deluge never slackened. He got up finally, with the water weighting the old blanket, and started in a direct, trudging way for the soddy. It was nearly daylight anyway. If the Burrowses were out there he'd have seen them by now.

His black hat, shiny with the downpour and his flesh chilled through the sogginess of his clothing, he strode down out of the night like a shadow. There was discomfort in his heart and savageness in his mind. He watched the ground as he went, knowing it was useless. The rain would wash away everything.

At the soddy's doorway he scarcely hesitated, but pushed inward and smelt the dingy mustiness of the place. Whatever it was, tomb, death-trap — it was dry. He cast aside the blanket and tilted the carbine against the wall. He slapped his hat sharply against his leg, and swore again. If they were out there they were welcome to one shot. No one who would keep to his trail of vengeance in this storm should be denied some payment. Thinking this grimly, ruefully, he got down the lantern and lit it, noticing how the wick smoked and thinking he'd trim it one day.

It wasn't until he was standing directly under the hook Will had driven into a ceiling baulk and crooked it to hold the lantern, with both arms over his head as helpless as a newborn baby, that he saw the silhouette of a man standing across the low, dingy room from him. Then it was too late to do more than look into the vicious too-wide blue eyes and almost groan at the foolishness that had placed him so.

They didn't speak. They didn't move. The rain beat a terrible tattoo on the roof that drowned out small sounds like Jack's heart making a drumroll within his shallow-breathing chest.

"Hang 'er up an' keep your hands where they are. That's good." The vicious blue eyes grew less cold. There was a sheen of deep satisfaction mirrored in them. "Turn around. I'm going to get your pistol, if you make a move I'll gut-shoot you."

Jack heard his spurs ring their soft small music. He stared with dour closeness toward a far wall. The gun at his hip was lifted away and the spurs rang again when the gunman moved back. "Turn around. Now then — what's your business here?"

Jack's anger was with himself. Fleetingly he could picture the vast disgust his father would have shown had he witnessed this ridiculous situation. He was a man trained almost from birth in the ways of guns and men — now this.

"I said what're doing here?" The gunbarrel was steady, like the slate-blue eyes.

"I live here," he said heavily. "Who are you? How'd you get in here?"

The blue eyes didn't grin but the voice did, ringing with a strong and youthful pride. "I figured you'd be up where you were last night. I kep' the cabin 'tween us. Now — are you Fulton's brother?"

"Where'd you hear that?"

"In town. Are you?"

"Yes. Are you a Burrows?"

The too-wide eyes with their unwavering viciousness showed a splash of surprise. "A Burrows? You mean Abe Burrows?" The look went flat with unpleasant humour. "I ain't, by a damned sight, and for your carcass it's plumb lucky I ain't, too. Now, you listen to what I'm tellin' you. Clear out. Saddle up and ride on. If you're in the Malta country day after tomorrow you're goin' ta get killed. It don't matter where you hide — in old Sheriff Marlow's steel cages, even — you're goin' ta get the hell shot out of you. Do you understand?"

Jack had no fear of the killer nor his gun. He had no fear in him. "I understand you. What I don't understand is who you are if you aren't a Burrows, and why you're warning me off."

The cold-eyed man drew his brows inward until a deep vertical line appeared between them. "You don't have to know nothing."

"Were you here last night?"

"I do the talkin' — you listen."

Jack's hazel gaze dropped to the gun. "I'll listen," he said, "and I'll also talk. If you're going to use that, use it. But I'm still asking — were you here last night?"

"You mean with Colt?"

Jack's bitter smile spread. He looked into the blue eyes. "That's answer enough. You were here; you saw what happened to him. Maybe you know he was trying to bushwhack me. Do you?"

"You're too cussed nosey, pardner. You just listen an' do like I tell you. Saddle up by day after tomorrow and ride out. If you don't, you're a goner. That's all I been waitin' half the damned night to tell you. Now move ahead o' me — and if you're feeling real fast, why just make a fault and see what happens." The gun-barrel waved swiftly. "To the door, pardner; right out through it."

Jack looked into the confident face. He turned slowly and went toward the door. The rain was dinning a mighty thunder on the soddy, slanting into it with a pummeling force that made the atmosphere vibrate with motion. He went past his wet carbine and reached a big hand for the drawbar, lifted it, threw back the door and stepped out into the merciless storm. The gunman cursed a ragged thread of livid words when the rain struck him, and waved with his gun.

"Around behind the shed yonder. Keep ahead o' me and don't walk s'fast."

Jack moved toward the shed; the rain slashed at his gaunt figure and crashed into his back. The gunman came behind him, moving far to one side in a crab-walk, squinting through the rain.

Jack heard the flat, muffled slam of a gunshot in the murky greyness with a sense of disbelieving and threw himself flat in the mud — rolling, twisting frantically in the slippery ooze. But he needn't have, for the gunman was face down — as Colt Burrows had been, as Will Fulton had been too, in this same yard — face down and making feeble little movements in the mud as though he wanted to crawl. His fingers worked without coordination, clawing, bunching up and squeezing until the slimy earth ran out between them.

There was no second shot, no sound of horses as there had been the night before. Just that one muted rifleshot then the drumming insistence of the drowning rain again. Jack lay where he was without moving until his lips were blue with cold and no part of his body escaped the dank soggy wetness.

By then the dawn was lighting the sky with a stark dismalness all its own. He lay on his belly with one hand propping his chin, looking. There was no movement. He squirmed around until he could see the gunman. He was still. There was more danger in lying there after daylight than there was in getting up. Jack crawled to the gunman, rolled him over and peered into his blue face with its twisted, dying look. The man was alive.

He scooped him up and staggered back to the soddy, kicked the door closed and dropped the shivering body on the empty bunk. Straightening up he gazed for a long time at the closed eyes and moving mouth. Then he changed his clothes and ignored the gunman while he dried his guns, cleaned them thoroughly and reloaded. He made a small fire in the little iron stove and let the heat knead his pinched flesh.

Standing there with the heat and new light making the day something clearer, more sharply defined than the stormy night had been, he watched the dying man. The sense of wonder in him grew. He went closer, stooped a little and gazed at the gaping wound high in the man's chest. With an unexpected gentleness he slit away the shirt and coat and laid bare the purpling flesh. There was no hope. The man would drown in his blood, shot in the lungs like

43

that. Oddly, his own shot had killed Colt Burrows almost like that.

He heated two blankets and laid them over the gunman, made a cigarette, some coffee, and had both. When the gunman opened his eyes they were rational in a way that showed the churning agony in their depths. "Thanks," he said softly.

Jack ignored it. "Who are you? Why did you tell me to ride on?"

For answer he got a question. "Who done that?"

He shook his head. "I can only guess," he said. "It came from east of the soddy."

"Burrows? The old —" It trailed off as though the effort was too much.

The breathing got shallow as the lower sacks filled with the trickling blood. The words bubbled past the pale blue lips. The eyes grew deeper in colour, almost black. The gunman looked steadily at the earth ceiling with its sagging baulks and rough sheeting holding the sod up.

"Who are you? What's your name?"

"Don't matter. They'll — settle with Burrows — for this."

"Who will?" There was no answer to that either, just the uneven rasp of the gulping breath, the dying weakness of the passing storm overhead and all around them. The sounds of little rivulets, somewhere, soft and liquid.

"No, they'll think you — done — it!"

Jack leaned over the gunman. There was a froth at the corner of his mouth. "Who? Tell me."

He was too late. For an awful moment the eyes swung with their darkening stare, unseeing but fighting for a lingering moment, as though the gunman knew Jack would be blamed for his death, as though in a final lucid second he saw and wanted to cry out against an injustice. Then he fell back and a freshet of blood cascaded from him. He died like that and Jack stood in abysmal helplessness until he turned away.

The sun blazed out with its fresh intensity, making the earth steam and pucker as though to throw off the puddles that were everywhere. Jack went out, holding his carbine like a third arm. He saw the swish of a horse's tail and went to the shed. The rain had made the rein-leather hobble pliable. It dangled now from one muddy pastern. The horse was dark with water, the saddle was soaked. With deep acceptance of his lot the horse was standing under the shed eating shreds of ancient hay he found at the bottom of the manger.

It was after he had removed the rein

hobble, scraped off the cloying adobe on a board and was putting the leather back onto the bit, that Jack recalled another thing that had a bearing on the dead man in his soddy: what the sheriff had said about events he might not even control. They would weigh heavily in his judgment by the local people, one way or another.

He finished with the rein, made a cigarette, stood within the shed with the sounds of expanding wood cracking around him and the smaller, more distant sounds of brush and grass straightening under the hot sun. If the dead man wasn't a Burrows, who was he and why had he waited so long for Jack to return? Why too, did someone want Will's place vacant?

An awful thought struck him. It might not have been Colt Burrows at all, but someone the dead gunman knew, who had murdered Will. No, at least Burrows had *tried* to kill. If he hadn't killed Will, at least he had tried to kill Jack.

He threw down the cigarette and looked stonily out over the drying land. Irrelevantly, he thought he would have a good hay crop. With a curse he cast out that thought and returned to the soddy. The sun was warming the place. He went through the gunman's pockets. There was only a tight little wad of paper money held by a thong, a knife with a keen blade, some silver coins from south of the border, and a balled up rag of a handkerchief. No letters no papers of any kind with writing on them. He got up and stood looking down at the man. There had been a gun. He went outside and found it. It was slippery with mud and wiped off, it yielded only two initials on the walnut grips. They were scratched roughly on the butt. "T.G."

He left the stranger in the bunk, swiped off the water from his saddle, bridled his big horse and struck out over the warming, slippery earth, toward Malta.

Riding with his tigerish eyes roving with a ceaseless watchfulness, he worried over what lay behind what he knew. "T.G." had been at the attempted bushwhacking two nights before. He had known Colt Burrows. Someone wanted Will's place left vacant. They wanted it vacant badly enough to kill to get it that way. It wasn't likely to be Colt's father or brother. They wouldn't have sent an avenger, or if they had, they wouldn't have sent him to warn off Jack Fulton. They'd have wanted him killed, not run off. What else was there? He squinted against the reflection of the sun off the dying earth. What else? Who had been the assassin this second time? Burrows?

It must have been a Burrows out there in the storm, waiting. A mistake — the rain might have distorted things. Perhaps the killer hadn't seen Jack at all, only the second man to emerge from the cabin. He had shot thinking he was killing Jack. He had seen the gunman fall. He had ridden off in the wild rain, exulting. It must have been like that.

But they were all only names and guesses. He had never seen a Burrows. He had only seen two men who were hostile to him. One dead, face down with a carbine slug through him, and this dying gunman with the vicious look. Names, shapes, echoing gunshots. Nothing real nor tangible nor solid.

He thought of two other ironic things. The dead man in the soddy. His own tale of how it had happened. It would be as weak as the rain-vision must have been to the assassin. And, somewhere, there were men who had sent this second killer to warn him off. When their gunman didn't return what would they think — do? Who would believe he hadn't killed this second man? It didn't bother him in that light so much as the knowledge that he would now have two distinct and separate sets of unseen enemies.

He saw Malta shimmering dully like rusty metal, in the distance. He drew rein for a moment looking at it. Any one of the men walking its streets could calmly, with no danger to themselves, draw a gun and shoot him in the back as he rode past. It was one thing to shoot a known enemy. It was another to be thrown into a maelstrom of hatred against men he didn't know by either name or sight. Two sets of men out to kill him for different reasons and he knew none of them.

He made a cigarette with his sharp, cold glance watching the cowtown shake off its rain like a wet dog, under the shimmering from the sunlight. He smoked solemnly, thinking that this was the most perilous, strange situation a man could find himself in.

Chapter Two

Heading down to Malta but by a devious way, he went to Amos Marlow's office leaving his big ugly horse tied out in back where he wouldn't be recognised. The sheriff met him with a harrassed watchfulness. "Now what?" he said.

Jack told him of the wild, storming night, of his vigil and the dead man. Marlow sat composed, listening, then he swore in a flat, hard way, throwing the words out fiercely.

"I warned you, Fulton. I told you what'd happen around here."

The hazel eyes showed resentment in their wary depths. "You told me people'd judge me by my actions after the shooting of Burrows. That's all you told me."

Marlow got up and walked over to the rifle rack and back to his table again. He stopped and faced the younger man. "Am I supposed to believe that's how this second one got killed?" He had an angry set to his face. "Who's going to believe that, Fulton? Listen, I told you what'd happen if you hung around. Now it's happened. Folks'll hang you higher'n a crow's nest. You come into the country and men start dyin' because of you."

"What I told you is the gospel truth," the gaunt man said evenly.

"Gospel!" Marlow said with rising anger. "Gospel hell! I know your breed, Fulton. Your daddies raised you in the likeness of themselves. Well, the West's changed from the Injun killin' days. We got justice and law now and we want it even better than it is — those of us who've moved ahead. Your kind is still teething on gunbarrels. Your breed trails trouble in its wake like a calf-killing cougar."

Marlow sat down heavily and worried up a cigarette with both hands. He went on speaking with a deep bitterness, without looking up. "Your kind goes where trouble is and makes more trouble. Well, dammit, it isn't going to happen here. Not in Malta."

"I didn't ask for that fight with Burrows," Jack said.

"Didn't you? You said yourself you baited him."

Jack got up and moved around the room. Anger was reflected outward from his face. "You're damn right I baited him. Did you reckon I'd sit up there and be a target? I knew he'd come back, whoever killed Will. When he came he was stalking me, or thought he was. Is there anything wrong in defending yourself?"

Marlow exhaled a mighty pall of grey smoke. "There's law here, Fulton. That's what I'm paid for; things like that."

"Is it?" Jack said thinly. "Where were you when my brother got killed? How could I have known Burrows was coming after me?" He made an angry gesture with one hand. "I didn't have time to ride down here after you, sheriff."

Amos Marlow was smoking thoughtfully. In a way what Jack said was right. He had the right to. defend himself. What rankled was this second one. The killing of Colt Burrows probably wouldn't have amounted to much by itself. Even the judge said so. But this second dead man out there . . . He wagged his head back and forth.

And Jack, as though following the sheriff's thoughts, spoke again, "I didn't kill this second one. Would I be here now if I had?"

"How're you goin' to prove you didn't? If he come with other men the rain's washed away the tracks by now."

"I don't have to prove I didn't," Jack said.

Marlow leaned forward in his chair and gazed up at the tall man. "The hell you don't," he said. "Listen to me. There's been three men killed on that claim. Your brother, Colt Burrows, and now this last feller. You're the only one that's living there and you're a stranger. How's *that* going to look to folks?"

Jack's anger was settling around his mouth in a hard, bleak way. "I thought of that before I rode in here," he said. "I also thought over some other things. The Burrows, for instance: I've never seen 'em. The men who sent in this second gunman; I don't know them either. I don't know any of the men who're trying to kill me. If I was making trouble for myself do you reckon I'd do it like that? Put myself in a place where I'm a sitting-duck for a passel of gunmen I don't even know? Would I have ridden in here and told you about this second gunman? Hell no! I'd of drug him out and buried him."

But Marlow had a deeper worry. It prompted his next remark. "Fulton, I've got trouble up to my armpits. You're only making it worse. Why don't you ride away from here like I told you before, and come back when your hearing is due?"

"*You've* got trouble! What the devil do you think *I've* got?"

"Smugglers," Marlow said drearily, "and you."

He leaned far back in his chair and looked

at Jack as though from a great distance. "The only way I can see for you, is if you go away for a while. As long as you stay around the Malta country, you're going to be in trouble."

"I'm not leaving," Jack said doggedly. "I came here for a purpose and I'm going to stick around until I find out what I want to know."

"Let the law do it," Marlow said.

Jack smiled with his mouth but not his eyes. "You've had time enough. Will was killed last winter."

"Listen, those things don't come out in a day. Sometimes not even in months. I sit here and listen and watch and wait. There isn't a killer alive who don't trip himself up if you give him enough rope."

"I don't have much time nor that much rope," Jack said dryly.

"You might have more rope than you know about," the sheriff said dourly. "Abe Burrows was in here yesterday talking war."

"Before the storm?" Jack asked quickly, watching the lawman's seamed face.

"Yes, in the afternoon."

"What happened?"

"We went over and talked to the judge. He said Doc told him Colt wasn't murdered. That Doc had found powder burns on

Colt's cheek and right hand which meant Colt had fired too. Also, Doc said Colt wasn't shot from behind and therefore Abe'd have to wait for your hearing before he could make trouble because it wasn't no case of murder; just self defense."

Jack had been listening with a thoughtful look. Now he spoke and there no longer was anger in his voice. "So, this Abe Burrows rode home by way of Will's claim with murder in his heart. The rain came up an' he lay out in it waiting to pot-shoot me."

Marlow pushed out his cigarette. "Who's going to prove that?" he said without looking up.

"No one, I reckon, but it fits pretty well, doesn't it?"

"How the devil would I know?"

"Well, how do you expect to find out, sitting in here and talking all day long?"

"Don't worry about that, Fulton. I haven't let many killings get by me yet."

"Where's Burrows live?"

"Why?" The faded eyes were piercing. "You want to ride over and pay a .30-.30 call to get even?"

Jack shook his head. "I have no reason to shoot him. All I know is that his son tried to drygulch me in the night. That's no reason to kill the old man."

Marlow looked sardonic. "Decent of you," he said softly. "He lives back in the trees about six, seven miles northwest of you."

Jack's thoughtful look grew inward. The place he had seen from up on the rock. That was the Burrows place. He recalled the ranch vividly but said nothing about it when next he spoke. "Can you guess who the men are that want Will's place left vacant, or why?"

Amos shook his head shortly. "I don't know nothing about that at all. That's your theory, not mine."

"All right. One more thing; do you know a gunman whose initials are T.G.?"

"T.G.?" Marlow looked at Jack in a vacant way. "T.G." He knitted his forehead in a frown. "There's Tommy Grimes. Where'd you get these initials? What about 'em?"

But Jack wasn't ready to tell that yet. "Who's Tommy Grimes?"

"He owns a blacksmith shop here in town. Sort of a funny feller. He used to be a rider for the cow outfits, then he got this shop and went to shoeing. He's done real well. Got a home here in town and nice matched team and a driving-buggy that'd knock your eyes out. I just mentioned him because he used to be quite a heller."

"He's not an outlaw though?"

The sheriff shook his head. "No. There was a time when Tommy rode 'er pretty loose and fast." Marlow studied Jack's face. "All right, let's have it about the initials; I'm no damned good at riddles."

"They are scratched into the butt-plate of the gun this second dead man used on me."

Jack watched the sheriff. Both men sat in silence. The sounds of the town were around them, muted. Amos kicked his chair around and faced Jack fully. He had a little puzzled frown on his face. "I don't believe you *did* kill that feller, Fulton," he said.

"Kill him? Why, dammit, I told you he had a gun on me and disarmed me clean as a hound's tooth."

Marlow's frown deepened. "By God, there's somethin' goin' on here. Somethin' . . ."

"What? What're you thinking?"

Instead of answering, the sheriff picked up a fresh letter off his desk and held it out. Jack took it, read it, then re-read one full paragraph and part of another one.

'There is reason to believe the major portion of this contraband is coming into the United States through your area. The Army has agreed to offer patrols for detached service when and if it can, but the current Indian troubles north of your area make this aid very uncertain. Therefore your office is under the strictest orders from the Governor to put every available officer into the field and end this threat to the financial status of the Territory and the Nation, and to the goodwill between Mexico and the United States, without fail.

'Unless immediate and productive effort is taken and positive results are shown, the Governor instructs me to inform you that certain changes will be made in your department in accordance with his powers to act arbitrarily in times of emergency, and . . .'

Jack handed the letter back and matched the sheriff's look of concentration with one of equal sincerity. "I don't understand," he said. "Is this Grimes a smuggler? Is that what — ?"

"No, no, I don't think that. It's just this." He slapped the letter. "I've got that thing to worry about and now you come along with this mess of yours. I thought your affair was just another grudge fight, but I'm not so sure now. There are things about it." Amos Marlow let it trail off. He sighed and fished for his tobacco sack. Jack waited. The sheriff made his cigarette but he seemed disinclined to say more for a while, then, when he spoke, there was antagonism in his voice.

"Put every officer into the field. *What* officers? I'm it. Where's Malta going to get the money to hire a permanent posse?"

"How about the ranches?" Jack suggested.

"Hell, they'd no more give up their riders than I'd eat my hat."

Jack felt a little pity for the sheriff. He stood looking down at the harrassed face. "Well, I reckon we've both got troubles."

"I told you that before. Listen, Fulton, why don't you trail off for a month or so? By then I might have some time to look into your mess."

Jack sidestepped answering the question. Leaning back, he caught hold of the drawbar to the door and gripped it. "Will you be around to pick up this dead gunman pretty quick?" he asked.

Amos stood up and fixed the younger man with a baleful look. He was slow answering. "Sure, I'll pick him up. Be around supper time before I can get up there though, I reckon. You won't answer my question, will you?"

"No. I couldn't promise anything anyway." He lifted the drawbar and pulled the door open. "Tell you what, sheriff, I'll see you at the soddy this evenin'. Maybe we'll both have thought of something by then." He went out and closed the door. The sheriff stood looking glumly at the panel, then he swung his head and gazed at the governor's letter. He swore, grabbed the letter, wrenched open the door and cursed his way across the road toward the judge's office.

Jack thought disinterestedly of the smuggling problem that was plaguing the Malta law, as he rode northwestward. By the time he was swinging over the uplands with the village far behind him he forgot the sheriff's troubles and concentrated on his own.

So the Burrows lived in that log house he'd wondered about, back in the far meadow beyond the spit of trees. He rode that way now, worrying at the peril he was engulfed in, trying to reason something out that would make sense. There wasn't anything to work with but the newly acquired knowledge of who the Burrows were and where they lived.

He rode slower after he was in the open country, heading straight for the forest again. He had no plan at all. He just wanted to get close enough to see the father and the son; get to know their looks so he could recognise them. That's all he had to hold to and, small as it was, it was something. At least he would know two of his enemies.

Vigilance alone would help him in meeting the others.

Riding warily he thought back to something his father had dinned at all the Fulton boys, down the years. "If ye shoot at all, shoot straight." The time was close, he felt, when that advice must be put to work.

He entered the forest and immediately, scented shadiness washed over him in a benign way. Riding slowly, retracing his former tracks as best he could, he was nearing the brooding out-thrust of rock when he heard the insistent, constant lowing of driven cattle. He drew rein and listened. It was a fairly large herd and they were coming in a westerly direction, off to his right somewhere. He shook his head in sympathy for the riders who were pushing them, for driving cattle through a forest is probably the most exasperating chore on earth.

He reined back warily and rode south until he was sure the herd would pass over where he had been, and there he dismounted, left his horse, gripped his carbine and strode ahead through the trees for a glimpse of the men and animals. It wasn't hard to locate the cattle. Their bellowing complaints were never stilled and several times he heard the shout of riders.

By the time he saw the animals though, they were turning obediently, as though gifted with intuition, and heading through a dense growth of brush on the lip of the hill where a steep downward spiraling path lay.

Surprised, Jack hung back watching. The cattle veered off almost automatically, as though they knew the rough path from long habit. He reckoned from that they were local animals being driven from one meadow to another.

The first rider he saw was a whipcord older man with a fierce dark beard shot through with grey. He had small, deep-set blue eyes like chips of ice, and a hooked, predatory looking nose. Instinct told the watcher he was gazing at Abe Burrows. There was a mercilessness to the older man that was stamped harshly in every feature. The second rider, bringing up the drag, was younger but of the same lean, wiry build. His face was clean-shaven. His mouth wasn't thin nor the eyes hostile, but there was bitterness in the features well enough.

Jack waited until they had ridden by, then he left his carbine against a tree and walked out onto the broad, churned path the cattle had left. Tho scent of pine-oil from the crushed needles underfoot was stronger than the smell of the animals. He stood for a moment looking after the herd, then, satisfied he had seen the men he had ridden from Malta to study, he turned to go back to his horse and found himself confronted by a third rider — a girl.

She was sitting there staring at him, as astonished at his presence as he was at hers. The moment dragged for both of them. He recalled vaguely that there was a Burrows girl . . . Suzanne.

"Who are you?" she asked coldly, watching him with a sharp, surprised intensity.

He didn't speak. The astonishment was slow to pass. It left an alkali taste in his mouth.

"Answer me! Who are you and what are you doing up here."

He was untutored except in the harsh wisdom that came with hard living and yet he saw instantly, and with a deep stirring, that she was very pretty. He saw her against the dark gloominess of his experience thus far in life and she reflected with a startling beauty. She was small and dark with a supple richness and vitalness to her, as he had too, but which was more vibrant, more outward, where his was almost hidden.

She was sturdy and full-bodied. The deep brown eyes had a look of softness that thrilled him even before he was aware of it. Despite the surprise and suspicion in her words, there was a slow mounting feeling that went with her low voice.

"Doing, ma'm?" he said quietly, watching her eyes and the swift flowing life in them. "Why — I was just passing and I saw that bunch of cattle go by — and I just watched 'em — is all."

"Who are you?"

"Well — just a traveler. Who are you?"

"I'm Suzanne Burrows, that's who I am. Now — who are you and what're you doing up here? Spying?"

"I wasn't spying," he said slowly. "I was watching those critters go by. You wouldn't want a stranger to just up and ride through your herd, would you?" It went over him with a sense of faintness who she was. It was like a low blow. It pained him when it shouldn't have. He turned fully to face her and stood nip-shot, looking. Her brown glance swept over him again.

"There's no worthwhile trails up here. If you're a traveler why aren't you down on the range?"

"It's hotter'n all get-out down there," he said truthfully. "I'm a little partial to shade this time of the year. Being a stranger around here I didn't expect I'd run into trouble up here."

The liquid brightness of her eyes seemed uncertain about him, and the bleakness mellowed a little. "What's your name?"

"Jack, ma'm. What difference does a name make?" It was weak but it was the best he could do on the spur of the moment.

The suspicion was gradually fading. The challenge in her face softened. There were dark-dreaming shadows and lights moving in the background of her eyes as she looked down at him. With no conviction, she said, "I ought to take you on down to dad." He waited in silence, admiring her strongly. "Where are you from?"

"Well, just lately I've been over by Malta. Before that — a long way from here."

"How long? What town?"

"Indian Territory. We didn't live near a town." He had no trouble getting around her questions although he wasn't more than casually conscious of his answers. Maybe she wasn't paying too much attention to the answers either. She was something he had never seen so close before — a beautiful girl.

He fought down the rising currents of his blood and looked at her for a flaw. There was none. He reminded himself that she was related to the man who might have killed his brother; was the sister to a man he, himself, had killed. Even that didn't cool the fire that grew to be a force under his heart. So long as *she* hadn't killed Will, the rest didn't matter. In due time he would take care of the other.

"Why are you so hostile?" he asked. "Folks travel around all the time. Everyone who rides through here isn't an outlaw, I don't expect."

"Well," she said defensively, "for one thing, there's a murderer lives seven miles down the range from us. We keep a watch for him."

"Oh?" he said softly. "Who is he? Who'd he murder?"

"A stranger. His name's Fulton. He killed my brother three nights back."

"Why don't you go to the law down in Malta?"

The brown eyes deepened in their colour. "Law! This is our affair. We'll take care of it our own way." She eyed him darkly. "You're lucky, stranger. You're lucky my dad or Mark didn't see you."

"I reckon," he said. "I expect your paw and brother're orry-eyed enough to shoot a stranger on sight. Don't know as I blame 'em, either — or you."

"I didn't touch the gun," she said.

"I reckon we were both too surprised."

"Mostly, I reckon, but — well — Colt's

been down in Mexico for five years. It wasn't like it would've been if Fulton'd shot Mark or dad. I hardly knew Colt."

"Oh," he said, seeing the solemnity of her gaze, which was disconcertingly direct; seeing also how round and hard, and yet soft she looked. Beautiful, even with the wilful jut of her jaw and the darkness of her brooding glance.

"Maybe I ought to take you down to Mark and dad anyway," she said slowly, dubiously, the flow of her words low and soft, one after the other, the sounds pleasing him mightily. He shrugged despite the quick warning that sprang up in his mind.

"As you wish ma'm," he said. Then he smiled up at her. The transformation was startling. He wasn't conscious of smiling, and the smile in itself was startling, for he hadn't shown the world more than a bleak grin in a long time. "If you lead, I'll follow."

She had a quick rush of scarlet blood under her cheeks. He hadn't meant it purposefully that way, but inwardly, in his mind, he had meant it exactly the way it sounded.

Her eyes flashed but, seeking words, she could find none. It was as though a great and frightening weakness had robbed her of the ability to rebuff him. The deep stirring warmth of his eyes made the blood flow into her face. It didn't help her find words.

"Let's talk a little, ma'm."

"Why?" she said almost sullenly. "What's there to talk about?"

"There's the country," he offered. "It's big. I don't think I've ever been in so big a country before. Back home in The Nations we don't have unsettled country like this any more."

She dismounted then, for his words hadn't been at all what she'd feared they might be. And he'd struck a responding chord in her heart, too; she loved Arizona's wilderness, and well she might, for she had grown to young womanhood in its farthest frontier.

"It's larger than you think," she said, avoiding his eyes, "if you've never been over it." She pointed to some faint, purpling mountains northward. "That's Apache country. My dad prospected over there years back, he says there's gold over there." She swung her arm due north. "Over there's the prettiest cattle country you ever saw. Lots of water from the snow run-offs." She dropped her arm and looked westward where the sinking sun splashed scarlet, like thick blood, over an endless sea of trees and hidden meadows where the grass grew stirrup-high to a mounted man.

"Over there, there's elk and a few buffalo and grass almost as tall as a man, and some Spanish ruins."

"Have you been over there?"

"Yes, twice. Once with Mark driving back cattle, and once with my father. We found a skeleton with part of an iron suit on it. It's called armour."

"Armour," he repeated softly, in his untutored state finding wonder at her modest learning and ability to name things correctly. Finding even more wonder in her vibrant, dark beauty. He knew, as a range wolf knows, what it was that was hurting under his heart and in his spirit. Making pain come with a short-breathed strangeness, cutting deeply. He marveled with an overwhelmed sense of awe that such a thing could happen to him, or happen to anyone so suddenly, so alarmingly.

". . . Down that trail you came over, but only once or twice a year and then it's always men to see my father and brother." She checked herself suddenly, biting off the flow of words with embarrassment in her liquid dark glance. "I'm sorry. I don't — I haven't had too many chances to visit with folks."

"I wasn't listening to all you said. Do you run a lot of cattle back in here?" He was working to keep her there. The cattle came readily to mind. He didn't care about them.

"We run five hundred head, mostly. We buy and sell. Dad and Mark buy skinny Mexican critters, take delivery down by the border and drive them up here where the feed's good." She pointed with her chin toward the back country. "And back there where the early feed is."

"Oh."

"That's why my other brother — the dead one — stayed down in Mexico. He scouted up herds to buy for us." She looked over his head at the sky and made as though to rise.

"Wait a little," he said.

"It'll be dark directly."

"Well, I could ride a ways with you."

A quick-startled look swept over her entire face, downward from her eyes. "No. Dad wouldn't like that."

"Not all the way," he said. "Besides, you said you had visitors now and then."

"Not now. Not when we're moving the cattle." She got up and showed nervousness by walking over to her horse and leading him to the brooding out-thrust of rock and looking down into the valley where an early evening was descending.

Jack got up and strolled over near, careful to keep away from the lip of rock with his body, but letting his eyes sweep the big valley in its shadowy gloom. Two men were standing down there by an old pole corral shading their eyes and looking upward. One, as Jack watched, made commanding, angry gestures with his arm. A call floated up. It was unintelligible, all but the petulance in it. Suzanne raised an arm and waved back, then she swung back toward her horse and faced him.

"I've got to go. They'll be mad."

He was tongue-tied and mute. He turned and held her stirrup for her then stood back looking up at her. "I wish you didn't have to," he said simply.

She shook her head down at him. "*I* wish I didn't have to." The words came in a rush as though propelled outward against her will.

"I'll come back — we could meet up here tomorrow again. You could tell me more about the country. We could visit. You're lonely — so am I."

She didn't ask him where he stayed. She didn't ask him anything at all. The excitement in her was like wine, it showed darkly under her skin and in the darkness of her eyes. "All right. At noon?"

"At noon."

She left him standing there listening to the hoof-falls of her horse as the animal moved swiftly over the crushed, fragrant pine needles. She went toward the steep downward path the cattle had taken.

He made a cigarette with slightly unsteady hands and smoked it looking at the ground, his thoughts and his soul in a turmoil. Something prompted him to bend and look closer at the trail. There was a clot of dark blood there. Puzzled, he knelt and looked at it. There was another a little farther off. He straightened up to his full gaunt height and scowled, walking slowly, watching for the blood. Some of it was fresh, or had been an hour or so before. It was drying now. It didn't all come from one critter either. He got down on his knees and squinted through the failing light at it. The drops would be at irregular intervals and sometimes as far as fifty feet apart. The more he found the more puzzled he became.

Finally he stood up again, smoking. There had been no freshly de-horned cows in the herd. There had been no small calves at all. Then where had the blood come from?

He went back over to the escarpment of dark stone and gazed down into the valley. There was a tiny block of orange light coming from the cabin. He wondered if she would tell them she had met a man up above the meadow: he doubted it. The cattle were bedding down, all but a few late grazers. They seemed content enough. He squinted harder, looking for any that might be lying on their sides. There were none. It was a puzzling thing. The blood came from a wound and yet the cattle didn't seem distressed as far as he could see.

Amid the gloom that was lying over the land, over the forest with its darkening sentinel trees, the cabin light showed clearer. He crushed out his cigarette and thought alternately of the inexplicable drops of blood — and Suzanne Burrows. Gazing at the tiny patch of orange light in the lowering night, he thought it was like a square of life and hope and something else, in the darkness of a lonely man's existence. He strode back where his carbine was, scooped it up and went back to his horse, mounted up and thought of the 'something else'. Of love.

He rode down out of the forest with his carbine balanced across his lap. Inwardly was turmoil such as he had never had before. His old brooding fierceness was there, the stubborness that held him in this land when death was stalking him everywhere, but deeper lay the strangest feeling he had ever known.

Away from her, the impossibility of what he was hungering for came swiftly and ruthlessly to him. He had killed her brother. Her other brother and father were out to kill him. With the power of fierceness in him though, he beat back the impossibility of it and locked the bleakness out of his mind so that only the beauty remained.

He rode through the twilight like that, his eyes brooding and hazel-hard, swinging like the eyes of a wolf to see everything around him, gauging the night and reining around scrub-oak thickets and sage clumps. Doing all he had been trained from birth to do in order to stay alive in a hostile country, and inwardly feeding his soul with reminiscences of beauty such as he had never known before.

Someday he'd have to tell her. The thought made him full of unrest. As full of unrest as he had once been full of hatred for her family. He swore aloud and pushed the eventuality away too. His big horse flickered his ears then plodded on with no more thought of his rider. The darkness wasn't as complete on the range as it had been back in the big valley and the forest, but it was deep saffron and full of bulky shadows until he came to a rolling rib of land that slanted downwards toward Will's soddy. He stopped up there looking out over the long run of country, made soft and mellow in the dimness.

Off on his left was a splash of lantern light. Until that moment he had completely forgotten his intention of meeting Amos Marlow at the soddy.

He let out the reins and the big horse went dutifully down the gentle incline, across the scrubby flatland where the pallor of his oat crop was visible, like a huge squared carpet, in the night. He saw the outlines of horses and smelt the cooking fire where two toadstool looking shapes were hunched over. His horse showed interest for the first time since leaving the forest. He quickened his gait a little and by the time Jack was dismounting, watching the hunkering men, the horse was alert to the smell of other horses.

Jack held his carbine lightly, waiting for the men at the fire to stand up so he could see them. One was facing towards him. That one threw up his head and stared. The other man, his back to Jack, swiveled his head without moving, squinting at the tall, gaunt shape. There was a tense silence in the yard. Jack felt it along the back of his neck.

"Where's the sheriff?"

The man facing him jerked his head sideways. "Inside," he said curtly.

Watching them both, Jack crossed to the soddy, ducked low and entered. Amos Marlow was sitting in the willow rocker. His hat was far back and his face had a preoccupied, strained look to it. He moved his eyes without moving his head when Jack came in, then he grunted.

"Where'n hell you been? We thought we'd have to camp here and track you come dawn. Figured maybe some of those phantoms you were telling me about had downed you, sure."

Jack leaned the carbine against the wall, drew up a chair and sat down. He fished up a tobacco sack and offered it silently to the sheriff. Marlow shook his head. "Naw, I've smoked so much today my mouth tastes like the barn floor. Well — ?"

"Well," Jack worked methodically at the cigarette. "I went up where the Burrows live."

"Find 'em at home?" Marlow said dryly.

Jack licked the cigarette and nodded at the same time. He twisted up the end, stuck it into his mouth and flicked a match. "Yeah. They were moving cattle."

"You didn't talk to them, did you?" Marlow's steady gaze looked startled.

"No. Well, I didn't talk to Mark or the old man. I was close enough to 'em to talk though. I'll know them if I ever seen them again. That's all I went up there for." He exhaled and glanced swiftly, dartingly, at the

76

bunk. It was empty. He looked down at the hot end of the cigarette.

"You say it like you talked to someone else. Did you?"

"Suzanne."

Marlow's steady gaze showed nothing but he never blinked. "The girl. How'd you come to do that?"

"She came up behind me before I remembered there might be three of them. It doesn't matter though. She still doesn't know who I am." A stab of pain went through his chest.

"They do a lot of cattle buying and selling, I've heard. Never been up there but once, myself. The country's full of those hideout ranches. Mostly, they starve out in a year or two. Used to be the Injuns'd find 'em out alone like that and raise hell." Marlow jerked a thumb toward the empty bunk, but said nothing.

"So I see," Jack said. "Where is he?"

"Sent him on back with one of the boys." Another jerk of the thumb, this time toward a gun lying on the table by the cook-stove. "Is that the gun?"

"Yes. Did you see the initials?"

"Uh-huh. T.G."

"Well?" Jack said, promptingly.

Amos shook his head tiredly. "I dassn't

say, Fulton. It might be a gun he got from Grimes a couple years back when they were both riding for the cowmen. Anyway, the man's name was Lon Colley."

"Outlaw?"

"That'd be doing him a favour. Yes, he was an outlaw all right. He was caught robbing travelers on the Florence road and sent to Yuma last year. He escaped. I got a handbill on him at the office, but this is the first I knew he was back in this country. I figured he'd head for some place else."

"Must've been something pretty good to bring him back here if he was wanted and known both, down here."

"Must've been," Amos Marlow said musingly. "That's what I've been doing ever since we got here and saw who he was and sent him back to town. Tryin' to figure what's behind him coming back at all."

"If you've got that figured out," Jack said, "then you'll be able to tell me why he tried to scare me off Will's claim."

"I didn't figure it out, dammit. I just came up with more headaches than ever." Jack crushed out his cigarette and the sheriff began to make one of his own. "Tell me again what he said to you."

Jack repeated the conversation as he recalled it. Amos lit his cigarette and smoked thoughtfully until the younger man was finished, then he looked over at him. "Now tell me how he was shot, again." Jack did that too, and the sheriff looked more weary than ever. "The drygulcher was lyin' somewhere east of the soddy?"

"Yes."

"Well, I remembered you'd said that, and before I sent Colley back, the boys and I combed every cussed foot of the country where a gunman would've laid that night and we come up with just exactly nothing."

"No cartridge case?"

"Nothing. Not a doggoned thing." Marlow held out his left fist and opened it slowly. "But we found this up near the sage clumps west of the cabin." It was a brass .30-.30 casing.

Jack eyed the casing calmly. "Sure. I can walk right to the spot where you picked that up. It's mine. That's the casing I ejected the night I shot Colt Burrows."

"Is it?" Marlow said thinly. "Listen, Fulton, you're in a hell of a spot. Look at it from where I sit. Colley's killed and there's no sign at all over where you say the drygulcher was. On the opposite hill though, we found this — and you say it's yours. Now then, two men're dead and there's nothing in God's green world but

79

your word to show you only killed one of 'em." Marlow dropped the brass casing into a shirt pocket.

"Hell, Fulton. If you'd said you'd killed both of 'em you'd be better off. Folks might believe the second one was self defense too, but this way, you're just making things harder for all of us. For yourself especially."

"Don't you reckon I know that, sheriff? Damn it all, don't you think — like I told you this morning — if I'd downed this Colley I could have hid it from you dog-goned easy? I *didn't* shoot the cuss. If there's no sign of the man who did, why I reckon the rain must've washed it away."

"Washed away the shell casing, too?"

Jack's eyes showed growing anger. "He could've taken it with him. Smart gunmen do that."

Marlow leaned back in the rocker and blew out smoke. "He could've. I'm banking he did, too, but I'm only the man with the badge. The judge and the law books and a jury might think differently."

"Well —"

"Well nothin'." Marlow silenced him bluntly, then he smoked for a moment before he spoke again. "Listen, Fulton, I got some problems in this mess I don't like."

"I don't like any part of it."

"Wait a minute." Marlow was having trouble putting his thoughts into words. He always did have and always would have. That was the main reason he talked slowly. "Look here, I got an idea and I want you to work it out for me." The faded blue eyes were as level as lake-water and almost as deep looking. "I want you to go back up where the Burrows place is and camp out up there."

"What good will that do? I want to catch 'em right here on Will's claim."

"*Will* you wait a minute, dammit. You go up there and watch those Burrows boys like a hawk."

"Why?"

"Well, for two reasons. One is that I want you away from this soddy. The other is I want to know more about something that I stumbled onto today by accident, before I came out here."

"What was that?"

"It goes back a bit, but the interesting thing is — Tommy Grimes and Abe Burrows are thicker'n grubs on a cow's back again."

"Shouldn't they be?"

"I dunno. That's what's stumping me. Tommy's a blacksmith. He's got a hell of a good business. Old Abe and his boy Mark deal in cattle. They're as different from Tommy as night from day."

"Folks pick their friends from lots of different businesses."

• "I know that," Marlow said testily. "That ain't the point. Lon Colley and Tommy used to be pardners. When Colley got sent away Tommy opened up his blacksmith shop. Now, Abe and Mark and young Colt Burrows buy cattle in Mexico and fetch them to the Burrows place, fatten 'em and sell them. Now then, about the time Colley run out of Yuma prison, why Abe and Mark and Tommy started running around together like a pack of coyotes, and young Colt never hardly came back over the line any more at all."

"I don't see anything there," Jack said. "Just that — whoa! The Burrows' drive those cattle over from Mexico, do they?"

"Yes."

"They're bought down there and have never been over here before?"

"I reckon. What'n hell sense would it make buyin' cattle on this side, drivin' 'em to Mexico then turning right around and driving them back there?"

"None," Jack said. "None at all."

"What're you driving at?"

"Forget it. It was just an idea anyway.

82

Now tell me what you want me to do up there, while I'm watching Abe and Mark."

"Just use your eyes. I've got a feeling, is all. Just a feeling."

"What'd you stumble onto in Malta today?"

"The Burrows wagon at Tommy's slag heap out back of his shop. Two men loading it with slag from the pile."

Jack frowned at the sheriff. "I don't follow you."

"That's nothing," Marlow said unpleasantly, gruffly. "I don't follow myself." He twisted in the chair. "Like I said before — I've got a feeling about these Burrows boys and Tommy getting so chummy all of a sudden. And some way, I think Lon Colley was tied in with them. Then, to top that off, by golly, when I got to thinking back on it, all this come about right after Colley flew the coop down at Yuma. Hell, I know it don't make sense, Fulton. You don't have to look like I'm loco. I know none of it fits together very well, but there's *something* going on and it's all I can find in my territory that doesn't ring true. I want to know what Burrows and Grimes are up to and you can cover the Burrows end of the country while I watch the Malta end o' things."

Jack was watching the sheriff's face

closely. "Are you sure this isn't just your way of getting me out of sight?" he asked.

"I already told you that's partly it, but the rest of it's like I've just said. There's a nigger in the woodpile. It's the only woodpile I can smell out that's got one in it, so I'm trying to chase him out into the open."

"What about the Colley killing? You think maybe I did that. What about that?"

But Amos Marlow's disillusioned face was alive with feeling for the things he had just put into words. He made an annoyed gesture. "I never said *I* thought you killed Colley. If I *did* think it I'd think you did the Territory a service. What I was tryin' to get across to you was that your behaviour around Malta — you a stranger and all — is influencing folks against you. That's all. Listen, do you think I'd of told you as much as I have if I thought you were a gunman, yourself? Don't be so thick-headed, Fulton." Marlow groped with two fingers inside a shirt pocket. He chased something into a corner in the cloth, grasped it and pulled it out. A small circlet of nickel with a star inside the circle. Two words were stamped severely into the face of the star: Deputy Sheriff.

"Here, don't wear it, just carry it in your pants pocket."

Jack took the thing with a curious glance

down at it in his palm. "That," he said levelly, "is the last thing I ever expected to have someone hand me in this country."

Marlow's face in the moonlit gloom looked pale. "*That'll* show whether *I* think you're a gunman or not. Now will you do like I asked you?"

Jack put the badge into his pocket with a hard grin. "I reckon," he said, getting up and groping for the lantern. "I'm hungry."

Amos got up. He grunted and went over to the door, gazed thoughtfully at Jack's carbine, then poked his head outside and called. "You boys fed?"

"Yeah, fed and rolled in. What you want?"

"Nothin'. Just wondered if you needed vittals." He turned back toward Jack. "Don't you breathe a word about what we've just talked about."

"I won't."

Jack made a little fire in the iron stove and went automatically about getting a meal for two, but his mind wasn't on it at all. He tried to work the things Marlow had said into some semblance of order. There wasn't much more than the sheriff's doubts and suspicions to go by, and he had strong doubts himself about the wisdom of a lot of what Marlow had said. Especially about the blacksmith and the Burrows. And Grimes' gun — that could be explained away a dozen different ways, all very plausible. He turned and dished out the food into two tin plates and sat down at the table with no particular appetite. Will's murder had no connexion with anything he was involved in now, as far as he could determine. He ate, and watched the sheriff draw up a bench and do likewise.

"Where does my brother fit into this?"

Marlow spoke around a mouthful of beans and potatoes. "I don't know. I'm guessing now, like I was before; but you might be right about someone wanting this claim vacant, and then I'd say that Lon Colley and the Burrows boys are tied into the killing of Will, some way." He poked a knife at Jack.

"Like I told you when you first came here. Will made no trouble and he asked for none. Why then, would anyone want to drygulch him?"

"No reason that I know of, but he sure as hell got drygulched."

"Yeah. Well, young Burrows tried the same trick on you and it backfired. That, more'n anything you've ever told me, made me begin to wonder about the whole damned thing being tied together some way."

"It's a mess," Jack said dourly. "A hell of a mess."

Marlow didn't answer that. His silence was more eloquent than anything he could have said. They finished eating, had a smoke, and the sheriff fell into a deeper silence.

Jack would have taken his blanket and gone out under the stars but he knew there would be no sleep. He thought of Suzanne. It pained him to think of her in the light of what he was going to do for Marlow. It wouldn't matter to her whether he came as friend or foe, however, if she knew who he was. The longer he sat in slumped thought, the worse his position looked. Not just with the girl but with the people of the Malta country.

And also with some men who were out to kill him or scare him off. After the death of the gunman, Colley, he had no doubts about which route they would take now, to make his brother's claim as vacant as they wanted it.

"You don't look real pleased," Marlow said suddenly, peering from under brooding eyebrows.

"Should I be?"

"No, I reckon not — in a way."

"In a way?"

"Yeah, remember what I told you when you first came to see me? If you made any

87

trouble I'd lock you up. I don't expect you thought then you'd have any reason to pack a deputy's badge."

"That's right, I didn't. But I'm no nearer to what I'm here to ferret out now, than I was then."

"Oh, I wouldn't say that. Look at it this way. We're pretty sure who shot your brother."

"Are we? Who? You mean young Burrows? I'm less sure of that than I was before. If Colley hadn't shown up with a gun, too, I might have thought Burrows did it. Now, I don't know."

Amos Marlow's hooded gaze held steadily to the tall, gaunt man's face. "Maybe you don't want to think Burrows done it, now."

Jack shot him a quick, cold look. "Why'd you say that?" he asked.

"No particular reason I reckon. Anyway, that's out of my line. The thing is, as I see it, young Burrows killed your brother. Why? Well — guessing, I'd say because your brother wouldn't scare out. Knowing another Fulton, as well as your brother, I can see where that wouldn't work too well. All right, Burrows shot Will. The ranch was vacant — search me what difference this stump-ranch makes! — but anyway they wanted it vacant and they made it that way. Then, along you come.

They saw you meant to stay. You worked hard making it look that way."

"That's right. I did it just for that reason, too."

"I know it. Well, they sent Colley to scare you after they let young Burrows have a whack at you."

"Funny way to do," Jack said. "Try to scare someone out you've failed to shoot first. Seems to me if I was doin' it, I'd work it the other way around."

Marlow cleared his throat and spat in the general direction of the door. His aim was no better than his force. "These are funny fellers we're dealing with. One thing's sure in my mind. This damned soddy's tied in some way with smugglers."

Jack looked dourly at the lawman. "You've got smugglers in your mind."

"Maybe," Marlow conceded, "maybe. How come then all these fellers who're mixed up in this thing are the same fellers I suspicion of having some sort of tie-in with Mexico?"

Jack thought about it for a long time before he spoke. It was just barely possible, at that. Colt Burrows, his own sister had said, had been in Mexico steadily for the past five years. He glanced over at Marlow. "How long's this smuggling been going on?"

"There's always been contraband going over the line in one direction or the other."

"I know that," Jack said impatiently. "This particular phase of it, I mean."

"I'd say two years, maybe. I date it from about the time Lon Colley commenced raisin' hell around here, but it really didn't get big enough to get the whole danged Territory excited over it until about a year ago."

"Then young Burrows bein' in Mexico might not have a darned thing to do with it."

"I dassn't even guess about that. I never had any reason to suspicion the Burrows boys at all, like I told you, until I saw them start pardnering with Tommy Grimes all of a sudden. Maybe I wouldn't have thought much about that, except that it was funny, until I saw who your second dead man was; Tommy's old pardner. Then, this business of your brother's claim and all that you told me fit it into a sort of pattern."

"I reckon," Jack said grudgingly. "It seems to fit together in some ways. Why don't you just up and lock up Grimes and the Burrows men and drain it out of them?"

Marlow looked scornful. "Fat lot you'd get out of any of 'em that way. You saw old Abe, you said. Did he look like the kind of a feller you could worry much out of?"

"No."

"Then we've got to go on playing cat-and-mouse until we come up with something solid."

"Like contraband gold?"

"That's more'n I hope for. All I ask is that you watch Abe and Mark Burrows, like a hawk. If they make any funny moves, come and tell me. Beyond that, like I said before, we'll give 'em plenty of time — lots of time — lots of rope. They'll hang themselves if they're up to anything illegal."

"That letter from the governor didn't read like it meant to give you that much time, sheriff."

Amos's eyes widened a little. He swore with lusty good will. "If you'd heard the town councilmen when they saw it — when I laid it on the line about hirin' three permanent deputies — you'd of thought we had all the time in the world."

"With me you've got four deputies, haven't you?"

Marlow shook his head. "Naw, the feller who took Colley back to town was the liveryman. He'll turn the carcass over to Doc, report to the judge and that's the end of him."

Jack fidgetted on his chair and frowned down at the floor. "How'll you contact me up there, if you have to?"

"Unless I'm 'way off, you'll see anyone comin' long before they'll see you. You hang around that rocky point up there. I'll send someone to that point. All right?"

"Yes. What'm I supposed to do if the Burrows ride out?"

"Follow 'em," Marlow said sharply. "Follow 'em, see what they're up to and come tell me. That's important, too."

Jack got up restlessly. "All right. See you again." He walked out into the night without waiting for an answer.

Chapter Three

He had a little roll of food in the old blanket behind his cantle and he wore his long dun-coloured coat when he wove his way back into the forest again just before dawn. He halted once, looking back. Some vague words of Will's came back to him then. "Arizona? They say it's a good place for willing men who'll work, Jack, with a richness to the soil and a kind climate and everybody too busy workin' and mindin' their own business to make trouble." Oh, what a lie!

His old brooding fierceness was back stronger than ever. It sprang from the torment within him. He sat without moving, waiting for enough light to come up to lighten his path through the dark forest. Everybody seemed hell-bent on minding everyone else's business — including himself, now. He watched the greyness come and give the land a bath in unreal light. He swung the big ugly horse and drove straight into the forest. He didn't want to see any more.

But occupying himself with the intricacies of the tree-gloom and the gianted boled obstacles didn't help much, because it didn't last long. His horse moved gracefully along a path he himself had tucked away in his small memory with all the vividness of an animal. He twisted and turned and made his way almost to the lip of out-thrust rock, then he stopped.

Jack got down, stalked with his big stride, a little stiff now with much riding and the slight chill of daybreak, to the stony prominence, and gazed down. There was the little square of orange glow as though it had been there all through the night, and, more surprising, there were droopy-headed horses, much used and tired, tied to the corral. Inside the corral itself were lowing cattle and two small figures he could barely make out, working as men work who have been doing the same job for hours.

"They don't even wait for sunup," he said aloud to himself, with wonder. "What the hell's so important about marking a new bunch of . . ." He never finished it for his mind had returned to the patient, experienced way the cattle had walked over to the little downward trail the day before, and had gone down it. As though they knew it by heart.

He hunkered, waiting for the light to come to the wide valley, hidden so perfectly among the pines and firs. He made a cigarette to kill time but he didn't light it; just held it cupped in one big hand. "Maybe they just never marked those critters before. But that doesn't make sense either. Not as old as some of those cows are; not in an open-range country. Now just what in the hell *are* they doing?"

He knew no more after the sun came up than he had before. He watched, puzzling over the way the two tired men ran the last batch of critters through a log chute and worked each one by hand, then let it out and barred off the next one.

He couldn't decide what they were doing, but one thing he knew they *weren't* doing, was branding or earmarking or wattling. Then what? What the hell else did these back-country Arizonans do to their cattle? There was no fire; none of the thick, cloying smell of burning hair and flesh that carried for miles even on a still day — and — most telling of all — the worked over animals didn't seem to bellow any louder than the ones in the corral. It was a puzzle that grew more and more bewildering as the shadows fell away down in the valley and the two men, turning out the last of the animals, dragged their steps toward the cabin.

Jack sat like an Indian, completely lost in

his thoughts for a long time, then he finally got up, lit the cigarette, smoked it for breakfast and went back to his horse. He rode in zig-zag fashion searching for a good camp site. The one he finally settled for was a long mile from the sentinel peak but it had water. One or two dry-camps weren't too bad but he had no idea how long he might be in the forest now.

He left his horse in a small park-like meadow along the creek and sought a deeper place for himself, where the water spread out on a slight incline, and there he bathed and made himself as presentable as his limited facilities permitted. As he ate a cold breakfast, he turned over the puzzle of the Burrows cow working methods. Then, with time to spare, he leisurely explored the country around his camp and northwestward, toward the place he was to meet Suzanne.

The day grew humid warm. Out on the range he knew it would be glazing hot with just the shimmer to give life to the country. He perspired too, but more with his depth of torment than the heat. He found the trail where the brush parted and went down into the valley and for a long time he moved back and forth seeking dried blood. There was more among the brush than along the open parts of the trail. Checking this discovery he went along the old cow trail first one side then the other, wherever the brush was, and sure enough, his suspicion was borne out in the churned earth and pine needles.

Whatever it was that made the cattle bleed like that, was aggravated by brush. That meant, he thought, that a great many of the critters had wounds on them. Not serious wounds for they didn't act like badly hurt animals, but wounds low enough on their bodies to be aggravated by the brush they rubbed against.

He went back by the escarpment, sat down near it but far enough back in the trees to see without being seen, and turned it over again and again in his mind. He was so absorbed with the puzzle that he didn't hear Suzanne until she was close, then it was the striking of her horse's shod hoof on granite that made him jump. He peered through the soft shadows at her, his heart beating a drumroll cadence that echoed inside his head.

She was early, he knew that by the slant of sunbeams where they came through the thick overcast. Watching her, he saw her lean over and frown. Following her glance he saw his own tracks around the places he had walked, and his heart sank. He could have cursed at the blindness that had let him do that; leave boot tracks up and down the dusty trail for her to find and read. The only excuse he had was his concentration on the strange discovery of the bloodstains, and that wasn't explainable to the girl.

She stopped her horse completely then, and the frown deepened. He got up, watching her, and went forward. "You're early."

She turned without surprise and looked straight at him without answering. He read the hostility in her dark glance, with no effort.

"I've been waiting up here for an hour or better."

"Have you?" she said, then she pointed with one hand at the ground. "Are those your tracks?"

He looked down, saw with disgust how clear and obvious they were, and nodded. "Yes'm, they're mine. I walked around up here. It's a good view." He forced himself to look over at her and hold his face blank and his eyes steady.

She swung down. He reached for the reins and led the horse back a ways and tied it among the trees. A raking glance showed the Bar-B-bar brand on the left shoulder. When he went back she was studying his tracks again. He felt like swearing. It was an awkward moment and seemed to last far longer than it actually did.

"What were you looking for, up there?"

"Just looking," he said.

She turned and faced him, studied his face with a long, steady glance. Then she said, in her low, rich way, "I don't believe you."

"Well," he said defensively, "I was here hours ago, waiting. I just walked around and —"

"And figured out how the cattle got down into the valley and back-tracked them a ways."

He felt his anger coming up and stifled it with an effort. Enough showed in his eyes to warn her though.

"Did I do something I'm not supposed to do?"

She dropped her glance. It swung to the out-thrust rock with a darkness he didn't like. "The rock doesn't show it, but I reckon you squatted out there, too."

He sought for a way to turn her suspicions or the conversation. None came ready to his mind. He shifted his weight and looked over at the rock accusingly. "I sat there for a while, yes. Ma'm — what's this all about?"

She swung toward him again. "What?

What do you mean?"

"You, the way you're actin'. You're making me out something sneaky. I don't like it, much." He found it extremely hard to be resentful toward her and his voice lacked solid conviction. The sense of guilt and deceit was very strong. It made him writhe inwardly.

"Then tell me why you came up here early? It isn't anywhere nearly noon yet."

"You came early." She flushed but said nothing. "Maybe we both came early because we wanted to. I — like I said — I'm lonely." That wasn't what he'd intended to say but the other words burned and hung up in his throat and made him deeply conscious of what his real reason was.

She lost some of her wariness. He could see it vanishing gradually as it had vanished the day before the same way. Despite some unwillingness on her part to have them be together like that. "I — you're a stranger," she said it as though it explained everything. It didn't, not to Jack Fulton.

"I reckon, but that doesn't make me a — whatever you were thinkin' a minute ago."

"It just looked funny, Jack. There — see how you went. Over to the break in the brush where the path goes down, then along one side of the trail and over to the other side and back by the path again." He heard the suspicion coming alive again in her voice and spoke out quickly, almost gruffly, to still it.

"All right, Suzanne, the next time I'll go to one spot and sit still and just wait."

She lifted her eyes to his face. They were dark and troubled. "I wish I was sure," she said.

"You can't ever be sure of anyone. I learned that when I was a button. You think you know a man: maybe you *do* know how he'll act when he gets mad or sees a gun on him or gets drunk. But Suzanne, I've lived just this long; all men are strangers."

"Do you believe that?" she asked slowly.

"Yes, I believe it. I've known a lot of men. In the Army and in The Nations. Cowboying and bull-whacking and stage driving. It's always seemed to me that you don't ever really know folks. Just when you're sure you do, why, they up and do something you'd swear they'd never do." He looked down at her with a haunting melancholy. "I reckon you'll come to see that someday. I hope not, but I reckon you will."

"Don't sound so sad about it. If a person turns out differently than you expected, it just means you have to study 'em harder to understand them. It doesn't mean they're bad, does it?"

He reached out and took her hand and leading her deeper among the trees, sat down with her. He wasn't conscious of touching her until he dropped her hand and saw the surging flood of dark colour in her cheeks. Then he was struck speechless by his own boldness and, try as he might, no more words would come.

But she wasn't lost for long. The thing he had been talking about was strong in her mind. "Well, does it? Does it mean they're bad if you find out something about them you didn't know before?"

"I don't know about that."

"Have the people you've known disappointed you?"

"Some of 'em," he said gloomily. "Most of them, I reckon."

"That's why you're lonely then," she said. "Because you're suspicious of folks. I'm not."

"No? What were you back there by the trail?"

"Oh, that was different. There was a reason for that. I mean generally I'm not suspicious of folks."

"Yes you are," he contradicted her. "You were yesterday and you were today."

"I told you, that's different."

"Why is it?"

"You wouldn't understand, besides I don't like to talk about it. Don't even like to think about it. It used to make me sick — really sick to my stomach. Now, I just don't talk about it or think about it."

He didn't push it. He didn't have to. She made it vividly clear to him that whatever her menfolk were doing, it was something she wouldn't welcome him prying into. Also, the way her voice sounded, it wasn't legal, or at the very least, it wasn't acceptable.

"Tell me more about the country," he said, prompting her to talk again, listening more to the voice than the words and watching her eyes, the way they would darken then grow lighter with golden flecks in them.

"I told you yesterday. There isn't much more to tell." Her gaze went westward and suddenly it darkened. "The range is down there. That's where that murderer lives I told you about. That Fulton."

"But *why* did he kill your brother, Suzanne? A man'd have to have a reason!"

"Dad said Colt was trying to cross his land coming home and he shot him down."

He was filled with a dark anger for her father. "If that's the way it happened, then I don't see why your paw doesn't go to the law. You can't go ridin' around the country shootin' men down without getting caught and maybe strung up. Why would he do it like that? There's no law against crossing a man's claim to get to your home, is there? Back in The Nations they'd string a man up who did a thing like that before his gunbarrel was cool."

"I don't know much about it. That's all dad told me. That, and the way he and Mark carried on."

"They maybe don't want the law meddling in. Maybe they want to down this Fulton themselves."

"They'll do it. We don't need the law to fight our battles."

"Suzanne, that's wrong. That's what the law's for."

"Not out here. We make our own law. Fulton'll find out."

He saw the flash of feeling flame across her face. It made his heart ache. For the first time in his life he wished he could get up and run away from something. She looked at him with a questioning gaze.

"Don't you think that's right?"

"If Fulton had killed your brother, what would you do?"

It struck him hard. He knew she had said it simply, on the spur of the moment and without more than a passing thought, but it was like a blow in the face. "I guess I'd do the same."

She was perplexed. "You just said I was wrong."

"I know it. I'm saying one thing and thinking another." *Doing another,* he thought. *Doing another. I killed your brother and want to kill again; if I find out it wasn't your brother who killed Will — my brother — I'll kill again.*

"I don't understand you, Jack."

He avoided her face. His eyes were moving with a rash of hurt and despair in them. "I've lived wrong, maybe. I was told that not long ago. There's got to be law other than gun-law. That must be right."

"Why must it? The law in Malta is an old man. He doesn't do anything."

"He does the best he can, I expect," Jack said dumbly, "and he's a long way from being dumb. Give him time. The law doesn't move fast. It can't. It's got to — to — wait, sort of." Everything he was saying was contrary to his rearing. He knew it and wondered why he was talking like that, echoing Amos Marlow.

"Let's not talk about killings and the law,"

she said in a small voice, seeing the turmoil in his eyes and the deep-brooding scourge that lay across his wide mouth and rust-coloured cheeks. She fell into a silence, watching him. It was as though a dark cloud was passing across his brow, casting a long stormy shadow over his features. She had never seen a man look like that before. Her father and brother were hard men. They either laughed or swore. There was no great depth to them such as there was to this stranger. She was fascinated and a little awed by him.

"All right. Tell me about the cow outfits around here. If I'm going to stay around this country I've got a lot to learn."

"Are you going to stay?"

"I'd like to," he said, looking straight into her eyes. "I'd like to a lot. It depends on a — lot of things — whether I do or not."

She dropped her gaze again. It fled along the ground and lifted at the dimly seen escarpment, soared out over the abyss where the valley lay and found a rest on the far distant mountains. "There are about five big outfits. Cow-calf cattle ranches. If you stayed, maybe you could get a job on one of them." After she said that she hurried on with descriptions of the ranches and even traced out their brands in the dust where she smoothed back the pine needles with a berry-brown, small hand.

He listened to the low pitched richness of her voice and watched the swift movement of emotions across her face — and wondered how Will had failed to find her, for Will with his laughing blue eyes and cornhusk hair had been handsome enough for her. He became painfully aware of his own drabness. His tall gauntness and brooding look.

Time went swiftly for them. A long slanting shadow told him it was late afternoon before she noticed it. By then they had an easy familiarity established as though they had known one another for years. It was strange that they never had a period of awkwardness, or self-consciousness, between them. There had been suspicion and even anger, then acceptance, and finally this smooth, swift-flowing familiarity. She looked up with a quick smile when the shadows were lengthening.

"Wait here."

He did, watching her move back toward her horse, seeing the sturdiness of her, the tawny wholesomeness. When she returned she had a bundle. It was food. Her face was alive with excitement as she spread out the cloth and showed him. He had never felt as miserable in his life as he did at that moment, with her kneeling across from him, looking up like a small child, eyes sparkling, waiting for his surprise and pleasure. He worked hard at it with the ache as solid as a lead weight in him.

She laughed at his clumsy compliments and his feigned pleasure. "Well, eat, then," she said. "Don't sit there like a sick cow just looking at it."

They ate with the hush of the forest all around them, then he made a cigarette and smoked, looking at her gravely. "Won't your paw or your brother wonder where you are?"

"No, I go out exploring a lot; besides, they're busy with the cattle."

It was as close as he could come to having an opportunity to ask her what they were doing but he didn't dare do it. He didn't want to do it, either.

"Was it good?" she asked him.

"Best I ever ate in my whole life," he said.

She bent to gather up the corners of the cloth and tie them. Her full mouth was quirked up at the outer edges and her brown eyes were golden with pleasure. He watched the sure, quick, knowing ways her hands moved and suddenly, from the great compulsion within him he reached over and took her arms above the elbows and drew her to him.

Suzanne was startled. For a flashing moment he saw her eyes; dark, troubled, frightened even, then she was against him. He found her mouth, but there was no response to it. Her body was stiff and unyielding against his. It was like that for seconds of fright and astonishment. Her lips were cool. Soft and full and cool. Then she responded a little, uncertainly, shyly, and he kissed her again, longer, holding her gently with a strong softness he didn't know lay in him at all. And she sought his mouth with her own and kissed him with a sudden fierceness, then roughly, almost clawingly, fought clear of him.

He felt a sorrowing peacefulness. It showed in his long glance at her. Her face was brick red and her eyes danced with strange glowing lights. "Jack," she said, as though more was to follow, but nothing came. "Jack."

He got up swiftly and leaned down holding out his hands. "Maybe we'd better go," he said dully. She got up and faced him, her lips parted in stunned wonder. Avoiding her look he took up the bundle; walking to her horse, he tied the bundle to the saddle and led the horse back. He held out the reins. She made no move to take them.

"What's come over you?" she stammered.

He looked impassively down at her. "Shame, I reckon," he said. "Here, you'd better go now."

"But I don't want to go."

"You'd better," he said stubbornly, putting the reins into her hand.

Her eyes darkened with a rush of hot anger. "Why did you do that, then? Why do you want me to go — now?"

"Suzanne," he said patiently. "It's best."

"Why is it?"

But he wouldn't elaborate, just shook his head and held out his hand to help her mount. She was trying hard to pierce the mask of his face and failed dismally. It was like looking at a wall of bleak stone. "Jack? Will you be here tomorrow — at noon?"

He considered it and found the desire to be with her too strong to deny. "Yes'm, I'll be here."

She swung into the saddle without touching his hand and sat up there gazing down at him in a strange and perplexed way, then, without a word she turned the horse toward the break in the brush where the downward trail lay, and rode off.

He walked down through the brooding silence of the forest without his usual wariness. Walked all the way back to the camp where his horse watched him with curious eyes, and sat down in the willow shade along the creek. There was nothing to say. There was nothing to think about except that he was deeply in love with her.

She had responded. That made it worse, not better. He smoked and sat like a boulder until the eating corrosion in his mind drove him to get up and walk aimlessly through the trees as though, through exertion and exhaustion, he might find solace.

He found no surcease from the anguish until the following day when he heard the faint, distant lowing of driven cattle. He stood listening, frowning. The noise grew stronger until he was alarmed by it. He saddled up swiftly, broke his camp and hid his effects, and rode warily through the scented shadow world of trees and dappling sunspots.

The cattle were going through the forest a long half a mile south of him. He dismounted, clutched his carbine and went carefully through the trees to watch them. It was the same bunch of lean cows again. Bony, slab-sided and shaggy, they nevertheless looked strong and wiry. He attributed that to the two days and nights of rich feed down in the valley.

The first rider he saw this time was Mark. The old man didn't come along until the drag went shuffling by; the slower, tamer, lazier critters. Old Abe looked as flinty and savage as he had before. There was a dark stealthiness to his bearded face. Jack waited until the old man was long gone, then he back-tracked the herd far enough to be certain Suzanne wasn't following before he went out over the trail and knelt, studying the strong smelling earth. Blood! He found it again!

A systematic search showed where the blood lay dark against the deep brown of old pine needles. It was still wet. He felt it, smelt it, and grew more puzzled than ever, until a determination came over him to find out just what, exactly, caused it.

He went back to his horse, mounted and followed the driven herd by sound. He let the Burrowses stay a good half mile ahead of him and he skirted their trail, never crossing it but riding slowly through the trees north a ways. The fresh early morning was on the range. He could see it through the trees now and then. From the sight he guessed they were driving their animals toward Malta.

Later, when the sun was nearly overhead, he was crouching among the last fringe of trees watching the strung out animals grazing their way leisurely north and west a little. If they held to the way they were going, they would cut across Will's claim. He stood up slowly. They wouldn't hold that way. They'd swing either north or south.

If they went south they'd be passing Malta. If they went north they'd have to go into the jagged rock country. He stared at the riders growing smaller. Colt Burrows' boots had been slashed and gouged by hard rock country. He remembered the boots on the man he had shot, as he stood there watching Mark and Abe drive their animals. Colt Burrows had shown the signs of the northward trail. He pieced it together slowly. For some reason they didn't want to drive their cattle within sight of Malta. Neither would they want to drive them through the hard-rock country. It would wear away the critters' feet like a rasp and leave them tenderfooted, maybe even limping.

If they didn't want the Maltans to see them and if they were afraid to have sore-footed cattle — then where were they taking them? A short drive on tender feet wouldn't hurt anything. He hunkered and made a cigarette and watched the men and animals become specks that seemed hardly to move at all in the immensity of land.

They didn't want their critters sore-footed because they weren't going to have a short walk ahead of them. That must be the answer. They were going to have a long walk — all the way to Mexico, maybe! He smoked and squinted against the sunblast, watching. His mind moved slowly, feeling its way. The reason they wanted Will's claim vacant was very simple, all of a sudden. Northward was the hard-rock country. Southward was Malta and observation. Will's claim lay between. With no one living there, Abe Burrows could drive his animals overland, bearing east, and bypass Malta, then he could swing south and make a straight, easy drive over the line into Mexico.

Jack snapped the cigarette. That was it!

Why? was the next problem. He shrugged irritably. Stolen cattle, probably. Whatever it was, he'd have to find out now. What had puzzled him so long was clear. Will had either stumbled onto what the Burrows men were doing or had been stubborn about moving off his claim. At any rate, Mark or Abe, or maybe Colt, had shot him in the back to get the claim vacant so they could drive their herds safely and unseen, to Mexico.

He went back to his horse and stood there, head down, scowling. Why? Stolen cattle? It didn't look right. He had seen Mark and Abe drive the animals over into the hidden valley. They hadn't branded them, they had done something else. Why would they drive them back to Mexico only two days or so after they had driven them up from there?

He stood lost in thought for a long time then a sixth sense warned him of the time. He swung up and reined toward the rendezvous spot where he would meet Suzanne. Instantly, he thought that they would be entirely alone now: the ranch down in the valley would be unguarded except for the girl.

He saw the opportunity and recognised the girl as the only obstacle. He racked his brain for a way to get down there without making her suspicious. There was no way that he could see. It didn't take much to arouse her suspicions, he knew that from experience. But this would be the best chance he'd had so far to explore the Burrows place.

When he saw her she had just come up the steep trail and her horse was still blowing hard. She looked even prettier than she had the day before. Her hair shone in the stippled light and her eyes had a liquid warmth in them. Her face shone and the deep colour of her mouth was like blood, almost. Blood!

He smiled over at her wondering more than ever about the blood along the trail.

"You're not early this time," she said pointedly.

His smile widened and the rush of blood to his face felt hot. Gosh, she was beautiful! It made him want to throw himself off the horse and take her into his arms and tell her all that he was; all that he knew. The surge passed swiftly, leaving him calm and aching as before, filled with a poignant hurt.

"Neither one of us are," he said. "I reckon we're getting so's we think about alike."

He led her to their shady place under the giant trees and tied her horse. She didn't sit down though, as she had before, nor did he. When he came back from tethering the animals she was waiting, watching his long, springing stride and the brooding impassiveness of his face.

"Jack? Why did you do that yesterday? Why did you kiss me?"

It jarred him. He had no answer and felt helpless before her searching look.

"I thought about it last night," she went on. "Do men do that — without thinking?"

"I don't know. I never did it before, like that. I don't know what made me do it, Suzanne. There was the — the — urge, I reckon."

"You didn't mean it," she said in a low tone, doubting him. "You just wanted to."

He shook his head dolefully at her. "I meant it. I wouldn't have done it if I didn't mean it, Suzanne. I meant it all right." The words choked him a little. "A man falls in love like that, I reckon. I don't know about other men — or women either — but for me — well — it just came like that. I knew it that first day I saw you sitting on your horse behind me there. I've heard of falling in love. I never knew it meant 'falling' the way it sounds, though."

"Now?"

"Now I know it does. Just like that. Falling in love, like you'd fall off a horse. Falling."

"I can't say it as well as you can," she said quietly. "I thought about it almost all night long. It scared me stiff, Jack."

"Why?"

"Well, I knew how I felt. I just prayed you felt the same way. I don't know men too well. Oh, there've been riders for the cow outfits come in here. Mark or dad usually ran them off, but I got to know them pretty well. They weren't out to marry me, Jack. I could see that pretty soon. But this is different. That's why it scared me. If you hadn't felt the same way I wouldn't know what to do."

"I love you, Suzanne, if that's what you're wondering. It couldn't be any plainer to me. I'd be asking to marry you, too, only —"

"Only?" She prompted him with her gaze growing dark with fear and forboding. "I'll marry you, Jack."

"You don't know me," he said softly, in a pained way. "You don't know me at all."

"All I have to know is that you love me and I love you. That's enough."

"No, it isn't."

"Yes, it is. If you're a rider — why, that's all right. I'll live on the ranches you work at, with you. We can take a claim maybe. I can work. I'm strong."

"Don't," he said harshly. She looked as though he had struck her, for a quick instant, then the russet flush spread in under her skin.

"All right. I've thought you might be an outlaw, Jack. You don't have to tell me. I'll go with you."

"What made you think that?" he asked, watching her closely.

"Well, you're hiding in the forest aren't you? You studied over the country and asked a lot of questions about it. Why else would you be studying dad and Mark's tracks like you did? I figured it out after I saw how you acted. Jack, I'll show you places back here where we could live forever and no law'd find you. We could get some cows and be honest folks."

He watched the lightening of her brown eyes. Saw the golden flecks flash as she talked and built up her own hopes with a wall of fast-running words. His bitterness grew tenfold. He shook his head at her. "No, Suzanne, it wouldn't work."

She stopped in mid-breath, staring up at him. The hope died slowly out of her face. It was like a knife being twisted in his flesh, seeing her bleach out like that.

"It wouldn't work out for a lot of reasons."

"Jack — why? What is it? Tell me."

"I can't tell you, Suzanne. I can't even ask you to wait until things clear up. There's nothing I can do to change a thing."

"Then you don't really love me, Jack."

He made a short, bitter laugh. "Don't I. Better than life, Suzanne. Better than I've ever loved anything in my whole damned life. That's how much I love you." He said it so fiercely she was awed at the thunder of his words and stood, fixed in place and stilled.

"I don't understand. If we're in love —"

"Remember what I told you, Suzanne? Men aren't what they seem to be. Do you understand now? You wanted to know if I loved you. You know I do — I've told you. Well, now you're seein' that I'm not what you figured I was. I love you and yet I'm a stranger to you."

"You don't make sense," she said in her low, vibrant way. "I can't understand, Jack."

"You will," he said. "You will because I've been thinking about something and I've got to do it, Suzanne. Before I do it I want you to believe me. I love you. Do you believe that?"

"Yes," she said slowly. "I believe you, Jack."

"Then," he said with a rising, shaking harshness creeping into his voice. "Then — look here."

He fished the little star with the circlet of nickel out of his pants pocket and held it flat on his palm. Pushed it toward her with a fierce hatred for it, and himself. "I'm here to keep watch on your men folk," he said.

Her face lost its colour slowly and the darkness swept into her eyes. He saw the swift, twisting change. The rush of stunned blood that came like rust into her cheeks and the black roll of her stare that lifted from the badge to his face. He heard her say, in her low, rich way, "I could kill you!"

He was braced against it. Yet if it had been a slash with the quirt that dangled from her saddlehorn it wouldn't have cut any deeper. He dropped the badge into his pocket again and watched her. "Just remember that what I told you is the truth, Suzanne."

"I could kill you!" she said with low, strangling fury.

He couldn't hide the anguish so he let it come up like a mask and settle over his face. He said nothing for a long while. They stood like that with the soft fragrance of the forest around them, then he leaned a little and plucked the gun from her belted holster. He shoved it carelessly into his waistband and raised his glance, nodding toward the horses.

"Let's go," he said, and led the way to the horses.

They followed the cow trail to the edge of the forest and there he saw that she had been studying the tracks. With a gesture he steered her out where the smashing heat leapt down on them with a hating energy.

The land lay cowed all around them. It was the first of July. The brittle light glazed the land and breathing was difficult except in a slow, panting way. He rode beside her in a deep silence, his face bent forward and the meagre shade from his hatbrim making it old and sick looking. Neither of them spoke until a gradual falling away of the land showed Malta shimmering far ahead, unreal, dirty and exhausted looking.

"Suzanne, there's something I haven't told you."

"You've shown me enough," she said quickly. "I wish I hadn't been so — so — blind before."

He fell back into his silence wondering if there wasn't an easy way to tell her. If there was, he couldn't find it. "My name's Jack Fulton, Suzanne."

He looked around and winced from the shock in her face, from the stiff way she had jerked up erect and taut in her saddle, staring at him with dry eyes wider than he had ever seen them. He winced and looked away and spoke in the dull way again.

"You can't ever tell about folks, Suzanne. That's what I was trying to tell you — warn you — about."

"Why did you do it this way?"

"God knows; I don't. I didn't want to. It just happened. I —"

"No," she said bitterly. "You're lying. You made a fool of me. You did it like that so you could learn things. Heaven will judge you." The way she said it made the echoes touch his ears like hot irons. "Heaven will judge you!"

"I didn't lie to you." He was being dogged and knew it and didn't care. "I told you the gospel truth. I asked you to remember it that way, too, and you said you would. I didn't lie to you."

"Fulton! You're the man who murdered my brother!"

He shook his head slowly at her. "I didn't murder him. He came stalking me in the night. I set up a dummy. When he shot at what he thought was me, I killed him." He leaned a little, in his sincerity, from the saddle. "If I had known what was going to happen later with you, I give you my word I wouldn't have even tried to down him."

"More lies," she said flatly.

He sat back again and looked over where Malta was growing larger, less mirage-like, in the near distance. When he spoke the words fell flat and hopeless from him. "I think some of the men of your family killed my brother. Did you know Will Fulton, Suzanne?"

"I don't want to talk to you. I don't ever want to talk to you again, to see you or hear your name!"

He tried twice more to draw her out. He couldn't do it. She rode beside him like an Indian. Straight, inscrutable, silent, a companion in name only, in all other things divided from him by a hatred so deep it couldn't be expressed. He couldn't see her eyes with their hot, fiery look. Their unnatural dryness seemed a sort of blindness, black instead of brown with a shroud of pain so thick there was no room for anything else.

He rode with her down the north stage road that led south into Malta. They attracted a little attention, but not much. Most of the people in the shade of the plank-walks were either drowsing or hurrying to find relief from the heat. They went stolidly to the sheriff's office and dismounted. He tied both horses then led the way inside.

Amos was just sitting down when they came in. He caught himself bent and stayed that way. His tired glance went swiftly from one face to the other, then, with a sigh, he dropped into the chair and tossed two limp pieces of paper onto the desk in front of him. He waited, seeing the expressions, reading more from them than one would think. Amos had lived a long time. He had a power of gentleness in him none suspected.

"This is Abe Burrows' daughter."

"I know," Amos said quietly, nodding at the girl. "Sit over there, ma'm, on the wall bench."

"I want you to hold her for a couple of days, sheriff."

"All right," Amos agreed calmly. "What's the reason?"

"The Burrows moved out a herd of cattle this morning about dawn."

"The hell they did. And what's wrong with that?"

Jack made a cigarette listlessly and lit it and exhaled smoke. He was avoiding Suzanne completely. "I don't know." He studied the cigarette for a moment. "They had a reason to kill Will. I watched the route they took with their herd. North of my brother's claim. They had to drive the critters through that badlands, over the rocks, or south, close to Malta. Will's claim, vacant, would be perfect for them. They could drive across it eastward, then, when they were out of sight of Malta, they could swing south and go straight down across the line into Mexico."

"So," Amos picked it up, "you figure that's why they wanted your brother off the claim and the place vacated?"

"Yes."

Amos nodded thoughtfully. There was a little gleam to his glance when he turned toward the girl. "What about that, ma'm?"

She stared at the sheriff stonily. The silence grew until it became awkward. Marlow's forehead drew into a puckered frown

125

and he looked back quizzically at Jack. "She deef?"

"She just doesn't want to talk, is all. I don't blame her in a way. Anyway, I want you to keep her here for a little while. The men are gone and now she's out of the way. I'm going back up there and see just what the hell they're doing to those cattle."

"You suspect something?"

"There's sure as the devil something funny going on up there, but from the top of that cliff you can't make it out. Maybe down around the corrals and the barn I can turn something up."

"Oh," Amos Marlow said, arising. "You've got something that looks good. Fine, tell me what it is."

Jack looked at Suzanne. "Blood," he said, watching her face. "Those cattle are leaking blood."

"What?"

He didn't look around at the astonishment in Marlow's voice, but he might as well have. Suzanne showed nothing, just the same stoniness of stare and feature. Jack slumped, acknowledging defeat with her.

"I watched them bring those critters into the valley. They corraled them and ran 'em through a branding chute, but they didn't brand 'em, sheriff. I don't know what the devil they did. That's what I want to find out. Anyway, the day they brought them, there were drops of blood on the trail behind them. Then, this morning when they drove them out again, there was more blood. Not as much this time."

"Hell," Marlow said throatily. "You can't drive critters that're bleedin' out, Fulton."

"They're not bleeding, sheriff. Mostly, it's just a drop here and there. A scab or a clot. Probably wouldn't amount to half a pint for the whole five hundred head, but it's blood and you notice it when they've passed especially where they've gone against the brush and trees."

"Blood," Sheriff Marlow said in bewilderment. "What the deuce does *that* mean? What *could* it mean? Are there any bull calves among the critters, broke horns or wattles, or the like?"

Jack shook his head. "No, that's what I looked for first. These cows aren't dehorned or even branded. Another thing, sheriff, the Burrows boys are driving them for Mexico. Two days ago they brought them into the country. I know. I was there when they came into the valley with them."

"Well I'll be —"

"Wait a second. There's the first thing I noticed about them. They've been up here before. Maybe they bought 'em in Mexico — I don't know about that. But I *do* know that no cow-critter drives through a forest as nice and easy as those did, and hikes straight for the one trail in the whole cussed country that leads down to the valley, unless they've been over that trail plenty of times before."

Amos Marlow put both arms on the desk and leaned on them, gazing at Suzanne. He looked puzzled and worried but not unkind. "Miss Suzanne," he said softly, "you could he'p us a lot if you'd speak up." She sat woodenly, looking past both of them. Amos tried again. "Look at it this way, ma'm. We'll get your paw and your brother. If you tell us where they're going and all, we can get them by surprise. There won't be any fight. If we have to grub up the information ourselves — why, there might be shootin'." He waited, searching to see how close he had come to striking a responsive chord in her.

She lowered her icy stare and fixed it on Jack for a second, then dropped it lower, to the lawman's craggy old face. "Who would you send after them?"

Jack knew why she asked and what she would say back when the sheriff told her. It was as though he was inside her mind, hip-deep in the venom that was there. He waited, watching her face.

"Why, I'd send Jack here. He's a good man."

"Yes, he is. He's a murderer. You'd send a murderer after them. *I wouldn't tell you if you tore my tongue out!*"

Amos straightened a little in his chair from the fury that struck out at him from across the room. He looked completely startled. Staring at her for a moment, he let his breath out softly, audibly, then he swung a long look up at Jack. It was eloquent with questions but Jack's face was closed and grim looking. Amos frowned and sat back looking from one of them to the other. He fished automatically, without consciousness, for his tobacco sack.

"Well," he said dryly. "That's that, I reckon." He made the cigarette and smoked it thoughtfully, then he got up and beckoned to Suzanne. "Come on, lady. You won't be t'first 'un I ever had in here, but it's been a long time."

Jack watched her go through the narrow door into the back room where the strap-steel cages were. His throat was as dry as dust. He was still looking after her when Amos came back into the room. "Sheriff, isn't there a place outside where you could sort of board her out?"

Amos sat down. The chair creaked protestingly. "Not safely, Jack. I'd be afraid o' it. Listen, I wanted her out of the way so's we could talk. Suppose I took up a posse and rode after those men of hers. Hell, drivin' cattle they'd be easy to catch up with."

"Sure they would, only what'd that get you?"

"The Burrowses," Amos said flatly.

Jack shook his head. "You'd only scare away everyone else who's mixed up in it."

Amos nodded his head. "I reckon so," he said resignedly.

"What've you turned up around Malta?"

"Oh, yeah, that's what I was going to tell you when I locked the girl out back. Tommy Grimes."

"What about him?"

"This'll stump you for sure. Recollect I told you he had the Burrows' wagon down at his shop loading cinders out of the forges in it?"

"Well, I remember you saying he was using their wagon to haul ashes or something," Jack said.

"That's right. He's got two men who shovel in the cinders from the forges. I tailed 'em on one trip. They go out about five miles from town and dump the stuff and come back and wait for another load."

"Shouldn't be much of a wait," Jack said, "if he's got the blacksmithing business you say he has."

"It's a longer wait than you'd think. That's where the funny part comes in. They work after the shop's closed in the evening, making one trip a day. Now, listen to this. They've been dumping that ash out there for a year that I know of, maybe longer." Marlow paused to gain an effect.

Jack looked impatient. "Well?"

"That damned pile's no bigger'n it'd be if they'd been hauling out there for a week. Someone's carting the cinders off."

Jack's impatience grew until he scowled down at the sheriff in an unpleasant way. "Lots of folks use clinkers to line walks with and the like. What the hell, Amos — you've been standing in the sun too much."

Amos smiled benignly. "Think so, do you," he said. "Maybe you're right. Only, twice now I've seen the same men come with the same freight wagon, load up ash and drive off with it."

"What of it?" Jack said shortly.

"I followed those boys halfway to Florence and watched them deliver their load of clinkers to a forge out in the middle of nowhere." Amos paused again, his serene smile wider. "They put 'em into another big forge and heated 'em white hot, let 'em cool after skimming off the top crush of clinkers. I spied on 'em from up on a hill."

"But Pete's sakes, Amos — why?"

"Gold, boy — gold."

"How do you know?"

For answer, Sheriff Marlow dug around in a canvas sack beside his chair and held up some dirty looking, dull yellow metal. The piece wasn't large and had quite evidently been chipped in great haste from a larger chunk. Jack took it and hefted it. It was heavy. He looked at it with interest. "Are you sure this is gold?"

"Yeah, plumb sure. I had it assayed after I stole it out of that Florence forge and brought it back to Malta."

"Well, I'll be damned." Jack handed it back, still frowning. He turned the thing over in his mind for a moment. "Where does Grimes get it before he mixes it in with the clinkers?"

"I can't find that out but it doesn't worry me much."

"No? Why not?"

Amos got up with quick, excited movements. Jack had never seen him show excitement before. His old eyes glistened. "Why not? Because I'm satisfied we're on the right track. Grimes is a smuggler. We're gettin' close, Jack. By God, we're gettin' close. We'll get the rest of it soon now. What tickles the hell out of me is that we're not fumbling around in the dark any more. Lord! What a relief."

"Maybe *you're* not, sheriff, but I am. Grimes is the smuggler but the Burrows boys aren't anything more'n cow thieves."

"That don't hold water, Jack. Listen to me. If they were strictly rustlers they wouldn't steal over the line, drive their critters up here then drive 'em right back again. I told you that before. Now — there's more to this than you can see — me either. I don't understand it at all, but I know this for a fact. Some damned way these men are all tied together. Don't forget it's the Burrowses wagon Tommy's using."

Jack brooded over the discovery of the raw gold and how it was transported out of the Malta country. "Sheriff, they're doggoned smart. Doggoned smart. Who'd ever think there'd be gold mixed in with clinkers?"

"No one," the sheriff agreed. "Once that stuff's mixed in like that, even an old desert-rat wouldn't know it was gold unless he sat down and really assayed it. Sure they're smart, but that's only part of it. We still don't know all of them or how they get the cussed stuff up here. In fact, about all we know now that we didn't know before, is that it's gold and that Tommy Grimes melts it in with the clinkers, at his shop — probably after hours — and has it dumped out on the range like slag. After that we know who picks it up and what they do with it." Amos's face shone with less enthusiasm, but his eyes still sparkled.

"Now then, you keep to your end of it and I'll keep to mine. Jack, I've got a feeling we're pretty close to kicking the lid off something pretty damned big."

Jack said nothing. The more he puzzled over it the less he felt he knew. For instance, why must Will's claim be left vacant, why was there blood on the trail, why had Grimes sent a messenger to warn him off?

He sighed wearily and crossed to the door. "Adios," he said, and went back out into the smashing sunlight. He took his horse and Suzanne's Bar-B-bar animal by the reins, and led them around behind the sheriff's office to a green-scummed watering trough. He stood between the animals while they drank, studying the town warily over their backs. Mounting up he rode west, away from Malta, until he was a good five miles across the range, then swung due north.

The heat was like the hubs of hell and the sun hung like a huge blood-blister in a faded, gasping sky. He felt it all right, but his mind was occupied with other things. Like saying good-bye to Suzanne. He had thought of it, back there, but he hadn't done it.

When the spit of forest came into sight he was grateful for it. The shade would be a blessing. More than that, he had the Burrows ranch to himself. He wanted that more than anything else, right now. When the scent of pines and fir came down to him he relaxed in the saddle and flicked away the sweat that glistened across his face.

The big ugly horse knew his way out of habit. He felt for the unseen trail and followed it. Jack didn't rein him off it until he saw the thick, coiled brush patch where the trail led. He urged the reluctant animal toward it. The horse, seeing nothing ahead of him, snorted and hung back a little. Jack reined up for a moment and sat still, staring down into the valley. There were a few horses and some straggling cattle down there. Aside from that the place gave off an aura of silence and loneliness. He thought of Suzanne and the little block of light he'd seen down there in the soft, purple evenings. He urged his horse down to the trail, over the edge of the escarpment and downward, closing his mind against her memory.

The valley was much wider than it looked to be. There was ample sign of cattle everywhere. The smell of them was in the low-hanging atmosphere of the ranch. The grass was tall and more trampled down than grazed over. He rode directly toward the buildings, for anyone who was around could have seen him coming down the sheer trail. Once he veered off and rode around some high-headed cattle but the animals fled before he got close enough to see anything more than the big, blocky Bar-B-bar on their left ribs.

He rode to the house, dismounted, tied the two horses and approached the building boldly. The door shook under his knuckling and the echo of emptiness came back to him. He lifted the drawbar and entered. Strangely, the place didn't smell of old food and stale tobacco like so many mountain-ranch cabins did. It was airy and clean. He brushed through the four rooms in a pained hurry, made sure he was alone and stalked back outside.

Over at the barn he found ample splashes of blood lining the log chute. He stared at the stains as though willing them to speak.

There was little else. Inside the listing old

barn, grey and dying looking, hung six complete pack outfits with cowhide alforjas thrown carelessly on the hay strewn ground beneath the sweat stained harnesses. There was some ancient chain harness with dust a quarter inch thick on it and several good looking saddles. The center of the barn was filled with a big mound of fragrant timothy hay. Nothing there. He went back outside and walked around the corrals. Little spots of black, dried blood weren't hard to find now. In fact, he saw them when he didn't want to.

Growling to himself he went back to the chute and went over it minutely, log by log. Nothing. He shrugged and went back to the house. Standing on the porch there, he turned slowly and looked down the meadow. Cattle were grazing in the distance, tiny red specks with white on them. The Bar-B-bar horses were edging up gingerly, sniffing at his own horse. He turned and pushed back into the cabin.

The smell of the forest was strongest in the back of the house where an airy kitchen was. He noticed with a pang how neat and scrubbed everything was, then he pushed out onto the sagging rear porch and studied the forest beyond. There were several trails leading into the trees but he ignored them.

A wall of silence hung over everything.

He went back through the house and stopped at the doorway of one room where he could catch a faint odour of strong tobacco and whiskey. Inside there was little in the way of furniture. He ransacked the place savagely and found nothing. With more exasperation than anger, he went back outside, walked over to his horse and mounted. He had found nothing and his hopes had been high.

Chapter Four

He left Suzanne's horse in the valley and hung the saddle and bridle beside the barn. After that he rode back up the trail and down through the trees.

The Burrowses had a long start on him but they were driving cattle. He came down out of the trees in a loose lope and held his big ugly horse to it for an hour under the furnace heat. Not until he did that was it plain why he rode such an animal. At the end of the gruelling gallop the big horse was hardly sweating. He was like iron in spirit and strength.

The trail shuffled grudgingly until it was a couple of miles north of the soddy. Jack was smiling to himself as he rode. He came to the lift where the jagged hard-rock country was, and there early evening caught him. He stopped and looked up toward the forbidding lava formations, reined his horse eastward and cut along the base of the wrenched up, tumultuous country, but didn't enter it. He didn't have to. If his reckoning was right, it wouldn't be necessary.

By twilight, when the sun was sullenly

drooping away in the heat shrouded west, he found where the Burrows' herd came back down out of the rocks and there he paused again, looking southward with a gleam in his eyes.

Straight as an arrow now, old horse. Let's see if we're right again.

He was thankful for the stealthily creeping shadows that came down across the range for they brought a film of shade to the daylight and eliminated the glare, even though they didn't ameliorate the heat very much.

The big horse loped off the miles in his easy-going way. Jack rocked with his stride and watched the wide tracks of the riders he was trailing, where and when they showed together, in the drag. It looked as though the father and son were riding together a lot, and that brought a smile to Jack's face. A frosty, knowing smile. Why shouldn't they ride together? These cattle needed no herding. They could have been turned loose and they still would have taken the same trail and followed it to the same spot below the border — the spot he wanted to find now.

The daylight grew into a mauve shadow that drenched the parched land. It softened, then deepened, and within three hours after he had left off skirting the badlands, it became a deep, inky darkness. By then he had the direction of the trail fixed in his mind. The cattle were a good six miles east of Malta. There was always the chance Abe Burrows took of running across stray riders from the big cow outfits. Jack smiled over that, too. Old Abe had built up a solid reputation as an importer of Mexican cattle. Even Amos Marlow had told him they were cattle dealers. He laughed shortly. The night swallowed up the sound instantly. It was a small discord in the hugeness he was riding through.

When the moon came up it was fat enough to throw out a soft radiance. Jack reined up and let his horse walk for another five or six miles. Cooling him out that way, he eased him into a natural single-foot that spanked off the miles again. He was making good time and in the pale light he could see the cow trail again. It wasn't as wide as it would have been had the cattle been strange in the land, either. He noticed that.

Riding with a fierce curiosity burning in his mind, he felt composed if not happy, but the monotony of his trailing bore in upon him later, after midnight, and he swung to other thoughts.

Suzanne . . .

The big horse was getting used to hearing him say things aloud. He hardly flickered his ears. "Why did it happen, Suzanne?" There was no answer and he sought for none. It *had* happened. Perhaps there had been another way he should have worked it. He considered that, too, and came up with the dire and grim knowledge that he would have had to tell her someday, who he was. She might even have found it out before he ever got around to telling her. No, even running, even throwing up his search for his brother's killer and riding away with her — under an assumed name, or something like that — wouldn't have worked. He recalled what she had said after the first shock had passed.

"I could kill you!"

He groaned deep in his chest and shook his head from side to side in an agonised way, while the land rolling south before him was like a faint carpet of moonglow spread upon Arizona.

Some men aren't born to happiness. His father had told him that — had told them all that — Will too. He had even said in his deep-rolling, thundering voice, that the Fulton boys had no right to expect happiness. Maybe he was right. He must have been right. Will was dead, Jack was despised by the only thing he had known in his lifetime that inspired such a depthless love in him he was surprised to find himself capable of it.

The brooding, haunting memories of his life came and went and left him riding with the melancholy look on his face that came so naturally to it, out of long habit. A man might love and be loved, but it must be a frail thing. A thing unsuited to The Nations, to Arizona too, apparently. A weak, soft, gentle thing that couldn't survive in a savage land. Well, he had experienced it and he would never forget it. It had been painfully beautiful. He had known it for two days — a day and a half — and it had brought up things out of him that he never would have believed he had in him. A tender gentleness, for instance — a blind-loving hunger and a quick understanding. For a day and a half he had been a stranger to himself. It made him stare thoughtfully ahead at the pale country. A man was a stranger even to himself.

And somewhere up ahead were her father and her brother. Of the brother he had doubts, of the father, none. Abe Burrows was a wolf. It showed in every line of him. A rawhide-and-catgut old wolf as tough as they came and as deadly. He shook out of his reverie and watched the cow trail meander past. He had killed one of her

143

brothers, now he might have to kill her father and her surviving brother — or be killed. He remembered his prayer beside Will's grave. "Lord, let me serve as your tool in your vengeance." It appalled him. He threw back his head and let the pale light reflect from his drawn features, the sunburnt skin as tight over the bones as a drumhead.

"A man comes to know things, Father," he said aloud. "He comes in his time to see how things are. I understand why it isn't good for folks to take their own vengeance and I see why it isn't good for me to be your tool in vengeance against Will's killers. Father, if there's a way out, let me find it."

He felt no humility especially, just the knowledge that two strong men were together in the night and one needed the council of the other.

The coolness came gently just before dawn. It was a blessing, too. Both rider and horse reveled in it as though they wished they might store up some of it against the cauldron-fire of daylight. Too, it told Jack how many more hours he had before daylight showed him glaringly, moving alone down the back-trail of the Burrowses.

He watched the greyness come and his spirit rose up in him to match it and meet it.

He studied the land and saw with relief that there were breaks in the country up ahead. Rolling land-swells and clumps of brush. It wouldn't do to be as close to the Burrowses as he figured he must be, alone, and be seen trailing them.

When he came to a swiftly rising rib of range he rode half way up it, dismounted, left the big horse to graze and went the rest of the way crouched and afoot. The musky odour of cattle had prompted the caution. It was faint and low in the air but it was also unmistakable.

From the near side of the rise he could see a long way south. Far enough to see a yellow boil of dust hanging in the pinkening sky. Beneath the dustbanner were moving animals. It was too far to hear lowing if there was any, but it wasn't too far to see a brace of riders lounging along, side by side, off to one side of the herd, out of the dust.

He went up onto the skyline and squinted into the distance. It had to be Abe and Mark Burrows. He squatted, watching them. For breakfast he had a brown-paper cigarette with the long vista of landfall, south, that was Mexico.

The cattle were moving wearily. He could tell that by fixing their location on the range and waiting to see how much they moved over a period of several minutes. Very little. They were tired then, and sluggish. He gave them a half an hour of steady study while the daylight brightened, then he went back to his horse, mounted and rode east of the herd, testing the winddrift with a moist palm.

Riding through the increasing brush and spiny growth of Old Mexico he unexpectedly came across an old road, sunken, all but obliterated with the passage of time and disguise, and followed it south again. It took almost two hours to put him up where he had a good view of the cattle herd. Then he was able to identify Abe and Mark Burrows easily, the former by his bushy beard and slouched, defiant stance, the younger by the way he did the bidding of his father.

The cattlemen had pushed the herd just about as hard and far as they dared. They hadn't driven them fast but they had kept up a steady, unceasing push right up until now. Jack saw why when he crept back through the fringe of brush and looked over where they were. There was a brackish, nearly alkali water-hole, with salt-grass around it where the cattle were milling. It was the only water-hole he had passed.

Abe and Mark had unsaddled their horses and turned them loose to graze with long tie-ropes on them. The two men were lolling, smoking. When they spoke, which was seldom and in one or two grunted words, Jack could hear the sound of their voices but not the words. The scene was a picturesque one. Cattle, tanked up on water and logy, grazing or bedding down, horses rolling to scratch the sweat-itch on their backs and the two men lazing. It might have been a scene taken from any cow country the full length of the Mexican border except for the watcher who lay prone, hidden behind a mass of flourishing mesquite, with a carbine in his right hand.

Jack gazed at the nearest cattle. Lean of flank and rib, they nevertheless were strong and wiry looking. The horses didn't look so good. They were tucked up and leg-weary. It showed the way they moved to and from the water and in the way they nibbled at the salt grass.

He got up and went back to his own mount, tightened the cinch before toeing into the stirrup, and rode leisurely on down the range into Mexico. There was little doubt but that the cattlemen would continue their drive straight south. While the cattle rested after the gruelling day-and-night-long drive, he meant to get around them and explore the country they were going into.

By the time the sun was climbing steadily and harshly up the ladder of little clouds overhead, toward its zenith Jack had made a huge detour of the Burrows cattle and had come back to his eastern parallel of them again. He was well in their lead too.

The land was the same for a long time, then he began to see breaks, great gullys and carved-out erosion ditches, deep enough to hide a mounted man, with a lot of room to spare. The country became more arid looking, with a few sahuaros standing stark and tortured against the warming skyline. Just before noon he saw the first habitation he'd ridden by since leaving the Malta country.

It was a great, sprawling rancho. The corrals, in that woodless country, were made of nearly straight mesquite shoots woven into wire and made solid and round so that no panicked animal could see through them and break out. There were several of these faggot corrals. They were much larger than any Jack had seen before, below the border. The place appeared to be very prosperous. He could see a couple of richly dressed Mexican *vaqueros* lounging in the shade with their ridiculously immense, peaked hats. The place seemed to be either in the grip of some deep lethargy, or else it was waiting for something.

Jack reined carefully away. He rode as far as the nearest and deepest ditch, led his horse down into it, took down his carbine and crawled back to a safe vantage point again. This, he felt, was the southern terminus of the Burrows' cattle herd. His excitement over-rode his hunger. He found a shady spot and waited. *

His most imminent danger wasn't from the *vaqueros* or from the Burrowses, right then, it was from the extreme warmth of the day and his own weariness. He had to fight off sleep constantly. Nor did the urge to close his eyes leave him until, faintly, he heard the coming cattle.

When they broke into view he was watching the Mexicans. They both threw down their cornhusk cigarettes, stomped them out and hurried toward saddled horses. Jack smiled. So indifferent, so lethargic and droopy looking one minute, so briskly alive and eager the next.

The Mexicans rode south of the ranch a ways and took widely separated positions out on the desert, waiting. It was a precaution they really didn't have to take, however, and Jack saw why soon enough.

The sun sparkled with sinister fervour off naked carbines in the *vaqueros'* hands. He smiled a little to himself at that, then looked northward and saw the Burrows' herd coming. As tired as the dusty, red-eyed and footsore animals were, they came eagerly, heads high in anticipation and their eyes fixed hungrily on the wide-flung gates that led into the faggot corrals. Jack's saturnine smile grew wider. These cattle had been here many times before, just as they had been down into the Burrows' valley north-west of Malta.

The critters finally broke into a shambling trot, lowing impatiently, hurrying to the corrals where they never hesitated, each beast crowding against its neighbor until the long flowing stream of red backs poured, gushed, and fought its way inside. Only the stragglers came without eagerness, limping, exhausted and dry-nosed.

When the last cow was in, Mark Burrows swung down wearily and went among the corrals closing the gates. Abe sat on his tired horse like a grizzled statue, watching the *vaqueros*. The Mexicans came riding slowly toward the yard, sheathing their carbines as they rode. Abe nodded in dour silence to them and a musical burst of border-English richly larded with Spanish floated as far as Jack's hiding place. All four men gathered together on the ground, led their horses into a shady part of the yard and talked for a while before the Mexicans took Abe's and Mark's horses and left the Americans to rest within the thick-walled adobe house.

The ranch drowsed in the nooning sunblast and Jack almost did, too. His eyelids felt as though sand was under them. He lay sweating in the shade, fitting this facet of the whole thing into its proper place. He couldn't see through the faggots that made up the desert corrals but he knew without seeing that the Burrows' cattle inside were gorging themselves on previously provided feed.

The sun drained the shade slowly as it neared its meridian. He hardly noticed. The Burrowses might buy cattle, he didn't deny the possibility. They must buy them in order to maintain their carefully established reputation as cattle buyers, but from what he had seen they were employed some way in an enterprise for which cattle served as a blind. Smuggling? It didn't seem to fit. Still . . . They picked up cattle down here in Mexico — at this same ranch more than likely — then they drove northward in a big circle around Malta, across Arizona's farthest reaches. The chances of being discovered were small, and even if they were discovered by riders from the big cow outfits, they had their reputation to extricate them from suspicion with. Clever.

Once in home territory they drove the critters to their hidden valley and up there they stationed a sentinel — Suzanne — at the only real vantage spot near their ranch, and did — something — to the cattle. After that they fed them until they were strong again, but not fat; then they drove them back to this ranch in Mexico by a circuitous route. It all worked out very smoothly. He watched the place with a glowering, unblinking gaze. But why?

If they were smuggling, it sure was a puzzler. He got up finally and went back to his horse. Riding in a large half circle and arriving back at the alkali spring, he unsaddled, washed his horse's back, drank deeply to offset the pangs of hunger, then went afoot back into the brush and slept with sweat running off him.

When he awakened it was late afternoon. The position of the sun told him it would be dark by the time he got back to the rancho. He went back anyway and hid, watching the place. Apparently the cattle had eaten all the provender put out for them because the two Mexicans were sweating and swearing as they forked great mounds of loose-hay over the far side of each faggot corral.

Jack had been lying there for an hour before he saw either Abe or Mark. Then it was the old man, his face washed and his beard combed, who came stalking out of the adobe house with his head thrust forward as though on the prod. Jack watched him with considerable interest. He stood sniffing the air for a moment, then he went over to a rickety platform, scrambled up onto it and peered down into the largest corral. "Give 'em more," he growled in a deep, throbbing voice. "Stuff 'em, boys. Don't spare on 'em, by God, they've earned it."

The Mexicans made no answer but their glistening faces showed briefly before they began to pitch over hay with more energy. Jack's little smile returned. He knew how the *vaqueros* must feel, as hot as it was. Before the moon came up there didn't seem to be much activity around the ranch, but afterward, with an immensely reflected glow of pale light rising up from the desert, Mark came out where his father was and the Mexicans ambled over to the Americans dabbing at damp faces.

Jack strained his ears to hear what was said, and couldn't. He decided to risk getting closer. But, for all it was night time, there was considerable light. He moved charily, crawling with sidling movements and keeping a lot of brush behind him as a dark background. It took half an hour to get where he could hear well and by that time one of the Mexicans had left the group, going into the adobe house apparently to make supper for them all.

Abe, with Mark and a wiry *vaquero* following, went over to the smaller of the corrals and clambered up onto the rickety platform built close against the faggot wall. "Like I said," Abe ground out in his deep voice, "they're mostly in the drags. Now — there — see that one? There, dammit. The one with the sore leg. She's too old. We can't use her any more. Take her out in the morning. Drive her a long way out and shoot her." The bearded face swung toward the son. "You know her?"

"Yes," Mark's low voice, a little like his sister's, came back to Jack. "I'll remember her. Any others?"

The old man didn't answer. He swung back and leaned on the faggots studying the contented animals with a keen, piercing look. "Take your horse and ride in among 'em. I don't see any more bad-legged ones but there were more in the drag today." He turned toward his son and the Mexican. "Any one you've got doubts about take her out and shoot her. Replacements're cheap and we can't have 'em falling out on the way back. Don't make no difference down here. Nobody'll stumble across 'em before they're rotted to bone, but over the line it's too dangerous."

The Mexican nodded soberly. "Just so," he said, "we are safe here. Besides, we have no one to fear." He flashed a dark smile at Abe.

Mark lit a cigarette and spoke without looking up at either man. "Wish to hell we could bribe our way into the clear up there."

"Can't," his father said gruffly, "and that's that. Don't need it anyhow."

"No?" Mark said, lighting his cigarette and blowing smoke out into the still night air over the corral. "If we could've we wouldn't have lost Colt and Lon."

"Colt and Lon," the old man said fiercely, "had nothing to do with the law."

"How do you know?" Mark said testily.

"How — damn you," his father said with mounting anger. "Because that Fulton's to blame — that's how — and you know it as well as I do. He's no lawman, he's a damned whelp, is all."

The Mexican saw their nervyness and tried with a wide, flashing smile to smooth them down. "I think things are all right, *Señores*. About Colt and Lon it is too unfortunate, but after all, we have become rich. Surely that is worth something."

"Worth nothin'," Mark said sullenly, "if you're not around to spend it."

"But you will be," the Mexican said blandly.

Mark's dark glance flashed to his smiling, serene face. There was scorn in the look. "*You* might be. We've got a bigger headache than you fellers have. Hell, you've bought off ever' Mex within a hundred miles of you. We've got no more protection now than when we started this." His voice held a strange mixture of melancholy and resentment.

Abe was scowling down at the cattle. Jack could see, from the way his mouth worked, that his mind wasn't on the animals, though.

The Mexican's complacency didn't waver any more than his smile did. "*Señor,*" he said quietly, tolerantly, "there must always be risk where there is huge profit, no?"

Mark subsided into sullen silence. He smoked and gazed frostily down at the cattle. The Mexican shrugged when he saw that Mark had no intention of answering him. He accepted Mark's silence as the answer anyway, and looked at the bearded, eagle-like profile of Abe Burrows. "Chief, the cattle look to me like they need a longer rest this time. What do you think?"

"The same," Abe said flatly.

"Then why don't you and Mark come down to Chihuahua with me for a few days. The rest would do you good. We all need a little rest, it seems to me." He said it with the faintest touch of irony but he didn't glance at Mark at all. Jack, lying flat, listening, appreciated the *vaquero*'s dryness.

"No time fer things like that," Abe growled. "They's work t'be done."

The Mexican studied the dark, forbidding profile for a moment longer, then decided against pursuing the topic and shrugged again.

They stood silhouetted on the pole platform, gazing abstractedly at the cattle for a long time. Not until the man called to them from the house did any of them move. After they had gone, Jack wormed his way to a better place of concealment, deep within the thorny embrace of a shaggy, tough old manzanita clump, and made himself as comfortable as he could.

They came back again just before midnight. Jack heard their voices before he saw them. All four of them were together now. The composed *vaquero* who had argued with Mark, leapt cat-like onto the platform

157

and waved an arm eloquently. He apparently was taking up a conversation they had been engaged in at supper. Looking at Abe he spoke in his clear, concise way.

"We could cut out all the old ones, every one we think might not be too good any more. Then we drive them into the desert where they could heal up without any mark, then drive them south and trade or sell them."

"Not too many," Abe cautioned dourly. "It's hell breakin' in new ones to go through the damned forest." He frowned blackly. "I don't like to take more'n fifty, sixty new ones at a time."

"But," the Mexican said, "you yourself said they were showing more hardship this time than ever before."

"I did," Abe answered him. "And it's the truth. We had to push 'em a mite. Without Colt and Lon to meet us down here and take 'em the rest of the way, we had no choice but to push 'em."

"We could find a couple more riders," Mark said softly.

Old Abe shook his head vehemently. "I'm ag'in that. We talked it over on the trail. Even if Tommy could find good ones like he says, I'm ag'in it."

"Why?" the Mexican asked.

"Because I see n'sense to splittin' 'er up any wider'n we're doing now. It's harder work, but we're getting more too, don't forget that." He shot the three men a harsh glance. "There's always the chance we might pick the wrong ones."

Mark sighed and moved a little, leaning over the corral gazing at the cattle, saying nothing. The Mexican was looking at the old man thoughtfully, also in silence, and the other *vaquero,* who had a brutish face badly pock-marked, and glowing small black eyes, neither spoke nor moved. Of the four men he looked the least intelligent and, with the exception of Abe, the most villainous.

Mark spoke wearily without looking around. "If we've got to rest 'em two days I reckon we might as well start cutting out the weak ones tomorrow."

"*Si,*" the Mexican spokesman said, following Mark's gaze toward the cud-chewing, placid cattle. "Two days cutting out, another two days marking — that should make them strong enough for the trip back, shouldn't it?"

Abe grunted his answer. "Yeh. Send Epifanio to bring in fifty head of new stock. The three o' us'll do the cutting and by day after tomorrow he ought to be back and we can commence loading."

The Mexican turned and spoke in a fluid, rippling torrent of Spanish to the brutish-faced *vaquero,* whose little black eyes shone wetly in the moonlight while he listened. He nodded and answered back in a husky, grating voice. The other Mexican turned back to Abe. "He says he has already made ready a little band of thirty-five and kept them apart on the range. Is thirty-five all right?"

"Even better," Abe said. "Have him fetch 'em in."

Abe turned his back on the Mexicans and looked at Mark's broad back where the younger man was leaning over the corral. "About this Fulton feller, Mark. We got to do something."

"Tommy said as soon as we got back with this load and he had a little free time he'd ride to Florence and look up a couple of boys he knows over there and have them cut him down."

"How much'll it cost each of us?" Abe asked suspiciously.

Mark shrugged disdainfully. "He didn't say. What's the difference?"

"We work for our money — that's what the difference is."

Mark looked broodingly at the cattle and

said nothing. For a while his father was silent, then he spat a dark stream at the ground and squinted his eyes tighter, looking out over the ageless, milky white desert. "I wish to God that claim had no one livin' on it. It makes the critters wear out twice as fast, takin' them up around and through those rocks."

"You should have tried to buy it from this second one," Mark said sullenly.

"Waste o' time," the old man spat back at him. "What'd the other one say?" Mark didn't answer and the old man didn't give him time to do it anyway. "He got hog-headed, too."

"Yeah, but this second one's hell on wheels with a gun."

The old man snorted. "Luck, Mark, just luck."

Mark straightened off the fence and looked dourly at his father. "The only time he was lucky was when you mistook Lon for him in the rain. That was pure luck, but when he shot Colt it wasn't luck — not the way he did it. That was damned coyote. This one's no greenhorn."

"Neither was the other one, boy," the old man said. "He just didn't catch on is all, and neither will this one. After we unload this time we'll see that he's taken care of, too, whether Tommy does it or not. We owe him worse'n his brother got."

"If Colt'd stayed down here," Mark said wearily, "he wouldn't be dead now."

"He wanted the five thousand," the old man said. "I told him we'd take care of it."

"We should've ridden on in again and killed him that night, instead of high-tailing it for home."

"How the hell," the old man demanded bitterly, "was we to know it was Colt and not Fulton that got downed? It sounded to me like one man firin' two shots like I told you then."

"We could've waited for him," Mark said, with the same bitterness.

"Are you short-headed?" Abe said. "Have you forgot what he said about leavin' him t'do it alone?"

"No, I haven't forgot."

"Well, then, quit blamin' yourself and me for what happened. It couldn't have been helped. If it's the last thing I ever do, I'll even up the score — but bawlin' over it won't help a danged bit."

Mark's brown eyes were fixed on the poles at his father's feet. He didn't raise them. He was long in his silence after the old man's outburst. The Mexican was looking away from them both, studying some distant point far out in the night with obvious chagrin. Jack tried to read his face. It was impossible from that distance. He flicked his glance back to the old man and kept it there. A growing hatred for miserly Abe Burrows was in him.

Mark finally pulled himself out of his gloom and looked at his father. "All right," he said, as though to dismiss the discord of moments before. "Tomorrow Francisco and I'll start cuttin' out the critters we can't use any more."

"I'll help," Abe said dourly.

"The three of us then," Mark went on. "Maybe Epifanio'll get back with the new stock tomorrow —"

"The day after," the Mexican interrupted. "It won't be so easy, I don't think. He has a formidable distance to go and much riding to go with it."

"All the better," Mark said. "It'll give us more time."

"If he don't get back by the time we're through cutting out," Abe said, "we can commence loadin' them anyway. It'll be easy enough with the old ones."

Mark frowned at his father. "We'd ought to give them a couple of days to rest, hadn't we?"

Abe shook his head irritably. "They'll

have two days and the fresh ones'll be easier to handle if they're leg-tired by the time we get 'em back into the trees."

Mark lapsed into silence again. The Mexican eyed him owlishly then swung toward Abe. "Who will you use now with the packs?" he asked.

"That," Abe said evenly, "is the only thing that's changed much. The way we had it before was neat — me and Mark bringin' the cattle, you boys and Colt takin' them the final leg o' the trip, and Lon doin' the packin'; but it's got to be worked out now so's we bring down the cattle and take 'em back, then either Mark or I'll have to pack down to Tommy."

Mark's brown eyes flashed fire. "Goddammit," he said savagely. "There's a limit to what a man can do. You don't think so but I do!"

The old man's wolfish eyes moved slowly to his son's face and stayed there. His voice went deeper, shook with an inner passion when he spoke. "We're getting right well paid," he said coldly.

"Yeah? When're we going to spend any of it? What the hell's the sense of working yourself to death, tell me that."

"You haven't lived as long as I have, Mark. There'll come times when you'll be willin' to work like a damned slave to make money. I'm makin' sure *I* won't have to do that again. I'm trying to make sure you won't have to do it, even." The fierce glance shone with Abe's inner ferocity. "If we can find the right men, maybe later we'll do like Tommy wants — take on two to replace Lon and Colt. Right now we dassn't. I got a feeling about things, right now."

"Feeling, *Señor?*" the Mexican asked swiftly, silkily. "How do you mean?"

Abe shrugged thickly. "Just feelings," he said. "There's things in the wind I don't like the looks of."

"For instance?"

"For one thing I'm a mite leary of this Fulton. Look-a-here. He was smart enough to bushwhack Colt. He deliberately laid that trap and got Colt in it. A feller that smart, is dangerous."

"You think he's the law?" Mark asked suddenly.

Abe shrugged. "I don't know *what* he is, but I don't like the way he worked that drygulching. He's up t'something. I know that from puzzling over the way he got Colt — and I don't like it. That's what I mean when I say I've got a feeling about things."

The Mexican was facing Abe, standing very erect. Jack got the impression of a man poised for flight, the way he stood there. "Then, *Señores,* like I said before, maybe we'd all better take a little rest."

"Yeah," Mark said softly. He was staring at his father. "By God, you're right. I didn't think about it like that. This Fulton is up to something. He must be."

"Don't get scairt," Abe said. "We've got troubles enough 'thout any of you gettin' scairt. Still, seems to me we can push through a few more drives. It's goin' to be hard work, Mark — you and me doin' all of it — but we'll make two, maybe three more drives, then we'll slack off for a month or two and sort of let the dust settle enough so's we can see what's goin' on around the country. We can work up something for Fulton, too."

"Maybe take a trip," Mark said hopefully.

From where Jack lay, he could see the sly expression cross Abe's face. He knew the old man was working to placate the boy, if Mark didn't know it. He also knew the old man was no fool. His last words had convinced Jack of that.

"Maybe," Abe said, watching his son. He drew in a big deep breath and exhaled it. "Let's fork 'em some more feed and turn in."

Jack watched it all waiting for them to return to the house. He was a little uneasy about having only three of them in his sight. Once, when they were coming together in the yard, on their way to the house, Abe turned and looked back at the *vaquero*. "Are your packs coming in like you expected?"

The Mexican spread his hands wide. "Even better," he said softly. "Where else can they get the guns and the bullets? Over the line there is too much Army; here it is different."

"You can't trust the damned snakes," Abe growled.

"I do, *Señor.* I have seen to it that they are taken care of. It's the cheapest good will we can have."

"You're good at it," Abe said with no compliment intended. "In fact, it's a damned good set-up any way you looked at it."

Mark turned back where he stood closer to the house. "Except for Fulton," he said waspishly.

Abe swung in beside the Mexican with a low curse. "Fulton be damned. I'll take care of him one of these days."

Jack smiled coldly, watching the burly back of Abe Burrows cross the yard and disappear into the adobe house where candle light spluttered into a steady orange glow. He worked himself out of the brush and went back to his horse, made a cigarette, lit it and rode back toward the alkali water-hole, lost in thought.

He cared for his horse and found a secluded patch of brush and there he dropped down. Sitting alone against a jagged growth of brush, deep in Mexico and peril, he stared steadily straight out at the moonlit desert. His mouth was drawn up a bitter slit. There was no doubt at all, now, what they were doing. He didn't know *how* — but that didn't shake his conviction. With the belief faded his most stubborn doubt — almost his hope — for the way to Suzanne was blocked more firmly now than ever.

They were smuggling. They were tied in with Tommy Grimes and those Mexicans. There was Abe Burrows' last remark before he entered the house. The things he said at last to the *vaquero*. They made sense only when coupled to the condition of the southwest at the time. 'Where else can they get the guns and the bullets . . .'

That meant the Apaches! His hazel eyes were dim with a veiled abhorrence for the men back at the rancho. The Mexicans paid in guns and bullets for the gold murderous Apaches tore from the blood-stained throats, purses and fingers of peaceful folks on both sides of the elusive border. They gave it to the Burrowses who smuggled it into the United States. Some way it was gotten to Grimes' smithy and there melted and mixed with dull looking cinders . . . It fitted perfectly.

He made another cigarette to placate the deep rumbles from his stomach and smoked it while he thought. He sat like that in the full circling solitude, piecing it together, and when his mind had fully grasped the depths to which Abe Burrows had gone in his blind drive for wealth, he hated the man more than he had ever hated anyone.

For Mark he felt contempt, but the youth's weakness, his underlying rebellion that came so near to the surface, made Jack's feeling for him less condemning than his feelings for the old man. And Suzanne — Abe had spoiled her life too. He had led one son to his death. He was leading another, if not to death, at least within the shadow of it. And he had built up a wall of dishonour around his only daughter that no one could tear down. For what? Apache gold!

Crushing the cigarette, he got up and paced restlessly up and down. It wasn't for a long time that the raging blood within him beat quietly enough for him to drop down and sleep again, not until the ghostly moon was dropping low and the far-off cry of desert foxes and sporting coyotes made a lonely, wild background for his thoughts.

When he awakened with the dawn he was resolved to ride around the ranch, farther into Mexico, in search of food. His hunger would no longer be denied. Before the sun had fully cleared the greying ramparts of the cordilleros, eastward, he was astride. His carbine lay across his lap with his right hand holding it and his reins were held listlessly in his left fist.

The country was all the same. Desert. He rode until almost noon before he found a faggot-and-mud-goat ranch worked by some beady-eyed Indians. He wouldn't have stopped there except that one of the prolific family was hunkering under a sagebrush setting a rabbit snare and so escaped his wary gaze until he raised up. Then Jack saw him and had no choice but to make friends.

The Indians gave him goat's milk cheese, dried goat's meat flavoured with pepper and ground maize, and their undivided, impassive, silent attention. He ate while the small black eyes of his hosts grew wide in astonishment. He wrapped up what he'd take along and put it behind his cantle, then turned back with a handful of silver coins. Only then did the Indians show a ripple of interest. He put the coins into the hands of the oldest man and tried stumblingly to convey gratitude but gave it up in the face of more inscrutability. Mounted again he rode due east — just in case.

From a brushy knob of ground he waited an hour, watching the mud *jacal,* but the Indians seemed already to have forgotten him. It was an unfortunate circumstance but there was nothing he could do about it now. He would have much preferred to find food farther away from the smuggler's rancho. He shrugged, lit a cigarette and turned back northward again. It didn't appear to him that the Indians were concerned over his presence nor interested enough to even be curious. Jack didn't know desert Indians.

They were as wily as the coyotes they called their brothers. They knew he would double back and watch them. This was nothing new to them, but it was to him. They ignored his visit completely and stonily, even among themselves, until he was many miles away. They were as canny as wild dogs . . . and treacherous.

Back at the water-hole he cached the food and took a bath in the alkali water, with the sun, at its fierce height, burning down. He rested again, ate more, then rode back in the late afternoon to spy on the rancho. He arrived in time to see the men leaving the horse corral where their sweaty animals grunted and rolled in sheer ecstasy. They went into the house and were there a long time. When they came out again, Jack was struck dumb by the sudden emergence of two familiar shapes around a corner of the larger corral. He watched the three white men freeze, looking at the newcomers. He wanted to swear, instead he groaned.

The damned Indians!

The Mexican spoke to them sharply. There was no suspicion in his voice, just a quick, knife-like intensity. It told Jack a lot even though he didn't understand a word of what was said. The Indians were friends at least, and more than likely employees living off the bounty of the rancheros. He watched them talking together. When Abe and Mark hurried over at the *vaqueros*'beckoning, Jack saw the older Indian hold out his hand and open the fingers slowly. The reflection of sunlight off the coins was enough. He was pushing himself backwards out of the brush when a rolling, brittle curse smashed the stillness.

He trotted quickly back to where his horse was. There was only one thing left to do. The smugglers were sure to be panicked now. Whether they knew who he was or not made no difference. They wouldn't think of him as a wayfarer; that was too much to hope for. Not in the state of mind they were in, now.

He rode in a loose gallop eastward, letting the furnace breath of the country leach away the perspiration from his body. Several miles away he halted in the stingy shade of a giant sahuaro. If he fled, there was a very good chance they might not go back over the line, either with their cattle or without them. For if they didn't find him, they wouldn't know it was just one man. They'd be more afraid than ever. He swore at his undoing.

If they didn't go back into Arizona, Suzanne would be forever in jeopardy as far as the law was concerned. Afraid of apprehension, they might not. Mexico was safety to them. He fished his pocket-knife out and poked it far down inside his boca. He dredged up the little deputy's badge and threw it as far as he could into the brush. With a look as baleful, as resenting and bitter as any his face would ever wear, he wheeled and rode south into the desert again, watching for what he knew would be a swarming band in search of him now.

It was a long chance and a dangerous one, but he had to take it. If they knew he was alone they might go back with the cattle. Beyond that there was nothing he could do except hope strongly they didn't shoot first. The hidden knife was all he could rely on now. It wasn't very much. But Marlow was depending on him and Suzanne was under suspicion; he had to force an issue.

Half an hour later he saw a Mexican trotting on a long-legged grulla horse, his head down as though looking for tracks, zigzagging through the brush. He turned a little so as to present a profile to the man and never once looked in his direction. He longed mightily to sneak a look but the best he could manage was a sidling glance.

The Mexican saw him and reined up sharply. Jack's heart beat fast when he saw the man slump a little to the right, then the sun flashed off a carbine barrel.

"Halt!"

Jack stopped apparently in sudden alarm. He looked into the gunbarrel and quickly threw up his hands. The Mexican kneed his horse closer, exchanged the carbine for his pistol and sat his saddle in what looked more like curiosity than wrath.

"Who are you, *Americano?* Where are you going?"

"Name's Peters and I'm on my way south — for reasons of my own."

The dark eyes glowed with ironic humour.

"You are a *bandido* perhaps? An outlaw?"

Jack didn't answer but he showed indignation which he had no difficulty feigning. The Mexican smiled and stepped down off his horse. "*Señor,* don't move." Jack obeyed. The Mexican lifted out his pistol and took away his carbine. He stared up at him with the same hard little smile then went back to his own horse, mounted and motioned westward with Jack's carbine. He could hear the Mexican behind him and rode slouched over, waiting for the rancho to show. When it did he reined up and sat there looking at it.

"That's right, *amigo,*" the *vaquero* said softly, gently. "Over there."

When they rode into the yard the place looked deserted. Jack got down slowly and frowned at the Mexican, waiting. The *vaquero* motioned him toward the house. He entered it with his eyes slitted to meet the gloom and coolness.

"Sit down." The dark eyes glowed with a strange friendliness, almost a triumph. Jack was puzzled by it. He watched the man put his guns on an old table and seat himself, holstering his own weapon. "We'll wait. My friends are still out hunting you."

"Wait for what?" Jack asked grimly.

"Who knows?" the Mexican said genially.

"Who can tell? Where were you going, in Mexico?"

"Just going."

"Ah? Usually one has a destination."

"I had a destination; Mexico."

The smile widened knowingly. "Over the line, eh? Running away?"

"I call it just making tracks."

The Mexican shrugged. "The same thing said differently. I lived in Arizona for many years. I know how they call things up there."

"Then maybe you know other things, too."

"Like what, *Señor?*"

"Like minding your own business and leaving travelers alone."

"Yes, I know of those things, but unfortunately we too, on this side of the border, like our privacy."

"I didn't encroach on your privacy."

"You crowded us a little, my friend."

Jack heard the horses coming. His heart missed a beat but it didn't show in his face. The Mexican arose and nodded his head toward the door. "Outside, *Señor,* and move slowly."

Jack arose and went out through the door and heard the distinct, sharp sound of a gun being cocked behind him. He saw Abe and Mark Burrows sitting their horses staring down at him. Neither man moved but their eyes bored holes through his body.

The Mexican spoke and Jack could tell by his tone that he was smiling again. "Here he is. It would appear that he is a traveler in a hurry to get over the line."

"Then," Abe said coldly, "he's got a posse behind him."

Jack was stunned. Until that moment he had thought surely they would recognise him. It hadn't dawned on him that they had never seen him up close. When they had come night-riding it had either been dark or raining. A new, fearful hope blossomed in his heart. He shook his head at Abe.

"No posse," he said. "I came alone. If there'd been one I'd of seen it. This isn't my first run for the border."

Abe's little fierce eyes burned into him. "Isn't it?" he said. "And just who the hell are you?"

"Name's Jake Peters," Jack lied smoothly, presenting a blank face to the men and hiding the real way he felt.

"Where you from, Peters?"

"Around."

Abe's chin jutted and threw his beard outward in a menacing fashion. "Don't horse me around, Peters. Answer up and damned quick!"

"From The Nations."

"What you running for?"

"For my health." He saw the quick rush of dark blood to Abe's face. "Matter of a stage over near Florence, back in Arizona."

The silence grew and grew until Jack could almost see it. The Mexican finally broke it with his shuffling bootsteps by walking around in front of Jack and looking intently at Abe. "I've been thinking; this man could help us."

"No!" Abe said instantly, thunderously.

Mark spoke for the first time. "Yes, he can help us at this end anyway. What harm would it do?"

"I won't have it. It's crazy. We don't know him at all."

The Mexican cocked his head to one side. A little flare of angry impatience showed in his eyes. "He can help us down here in Mexico. Later, if we like him, he could go north and help up there."

Abe's eyes were furious. They were doubling up on him and Mark's defiance enraged him more than anything else. Jack could see that, and felt thankful for it at the same time. He had become a secondary issue very suddenly, and the knowledge that none of them knew who he was became more than hope. It became also a grim jest that pleased him mightily.

He frowned at Abe. "Help you do what? What the hell're you idiots talking about? I ain't helping no one do anything if I've got to go back over the line to do it, and that's final."

It was a good stroke. Abe's granite stare turned gradually speculative. He looked for a long time at Jack, then swung his glance to the Mexican. "Francisco, you'll be responsible for him all the time we're gone. You'll be personally responsible."

The Mexican turned slowly and regarded Jack with troubled eyes, then, with the customary shrug of his race, he turned back and smiled apologetically. "It was a good idea, I thought," he said. "Still — one never knows."

"Keep him unarmed, Francisco," Mark said, refusing for any reason to alter the only defiant stand he'd ever taken against his father.

The Mexican considered that, then nodded his head. "It shall be so, but being responsible for him means I'll have to live with him. I don't know —"

"More than that," Abe said grimly, frowning at the *vaquero*. "You'll have to watch him day and night. If you want to keep him, on those terms, go ahead." He flung off his horse in obvious anger and refused to look at his son.

Mark looked just as grim as his father did. "Chain him up at night, Francisco," he said. "Keep him leg-ironed when you don't want to bother with him, but we sure as hell need another hand. He might turn out to be the one we're looking for."

"We're looking for no one!" Abe said wrathfully, leading his horse back to the corral. "Mark, you ride back and see if he's lying about the posse."

Mark stared hard at the old man. Jack could see the flat, thin slit of his mouth and the latent burning in his eyes. He waited for the explosion that never came. Mark jerked his horse around and rode out of the yard. The Mexican turned with a rueful expression and motioned for Jack to follow him. Moving toward the corrals he flung a look back where Abe was unsaddling. "Are you ready to work cattle?"

"I'll be there," Abe said shortly, flinging down the leather and leading the sweaty animal toward a faggot corral, growling under his breath.

By the time Abe came down to them, Francisco had shown Jack the reinforced cattle chute made inside one of the corrals. Beyond the chute was another very large corral, empty. "When we are finished with the animal we let it out into this other corral. Understand?"

"I understand that much of what we're going to do. Where are the branding irons?" He was looking past Francisco when he said it, straight at Abe Burrows. For the first time, he saw harsh humour show in the older man's face. It was gone in a second.

"We don't brand 'em, Peters." Abe turned to the Mexican. "Go fetch the first sack. We might as well commence loading 'em." They stood alone watching the *vaquero* go back toward the house. Jack turned his head slowly and found Abe staring at him. "You ever been up around Malta?"

"In Arizona?" Jack asked.

"Yeh."

"Can't say as I have. What about it?"

"Nothing," Abe said shortly. "You got a sharp knife?"

"No; no knife, sharp or otherwise."

"What's the matter, don't you Indian Territory cowboys carry knives? 'Fraid you might fall on 'em?"

Jack flushed with a brooding anger. "We're no more afraid of knives than you are of razors," he said coldly, eyeing Abe's beard.

Abe Burrows swung with a wild curse and

took two short, solid steps closer to Jack. "I'll break your scrawny neck!"

"Not from over there, you won't. If you don't want to get the waddin' kicked out of you, watch your damned mouth."

Burrows was purpling with a scarcely controlled fury when the Mexican came back into the corral. "What has happened, boys?" He shot them both startled looks and dropped a heavy canvas sack with a grunt.

"I got a notion to gut-shoot this . . ."

"That'd be about the way you'd do it," Jack said nastily. "You armed and me unarmed. Take the gun off and try it, whiskers." He was beyond caring. The hatred he felt was smothering him.

"Stop it!" The Mexican stepped between them with his teeth showing in a snarl and his dark eyes savage looking. "There's too much work to be done to waste sweat like this. You are fools!" He thrust out a stiff, wiry arm. "There — there is the gold. Let's get to work."

Abe strode furiously up toward the front of the chute. Jack watched him, moving so he wouldn't be flanked, then he turned to the Mexican. "He asked me if I had a knife and when I said I didn't he got all hostile."

"Over a knife?" the Mexican said in huge bewilderment. "Here — here are two of them, *Señor*, take your pick." He had drawn them from his waistband; wicked stilettos with gleaming blades and heavy handles. Jack took one and felt its edge. It was like glass. He held the thing looking at the Mexican.

"There is a long pole over there — yes — on the fence. Use that to drive the cattle into the chute." Francisco bent, took up the sack and walked angrily after Abe Burrows.

Jack, more mystified than ever, did as he was told. He kept the chute full of cattle and didn't have a chance to see what the *vaquero* and Abe Burrows were doing until the Mexican, sweating profusely and swiping his forehead with a bloody hand, motioned for him to come forward. He closed the gate to the chute and ambled through the burning yellow dust.

"Jake, Abe's going to the house and get us a pan of water. I will show you what to do. Tomorrow we will have more than enough to do for all of us."

The Mexican ran another animal into the chute, locked the tail-gate and bent low. Jack watched in amazement when he reached through the stout oaken bars and made a neat incision in the critter's hide under the brisket, back a ways from the front legs. He then fleshed the skin away

183

from the muscle with a long, graceful, sideways motion of his knife and stood up looking at Jack. "Do you see how this is done?"

"Yeah, only I don't see why."

Francisco flashed him a dazzling smile and dipped his hand into the canvas sack at his feet. Jack saw it glisten with a sullen dullness — gold! Refined, gravel-fine pieces of gold! He looked up swiftly to the *vaquero's* face and saw the laughter coming. From that he knew how his astonishment must look on his face.

The blood on the trail — where they walked in the brush! Good Lord! It made him want to stagger, for it all was clear in that one blinding moment. What Abe and Mark did up in their home corrals was open those pouches in the living hide of the cattle, scoop out the grains of gold — and turn the cattle out again!

"You look like a man who sees a ghost, my friend," Francisco said with a soft laugh. "Now watch how this is done." He bent swiftly and with the dexterity bought of much practice, he pushed the gold gravel into the little pouch he had made in the cow's undersides, pinched the slit closed and stood up. The pouch was deep enough and slanting downwards enough to hold the

184

gold perfectly. Also, as the little cut healed, the gold was further protected against falling out when the animal moved.

"But — doesn't it fall out?"

"How?" Francisco asked blandly. "We lose a little, but it is so little, *amigo*." He shrugged with a deprecating smile. His eyes sparkled as he watched Jack's face and he laughed again. "Come closer. I will show you once more then you will show me. It is a very simple thing. You take the loose flesh — so — cut so — flesh it a little — so — it is really a simple thing."

"Well, I'll be damned to hell."

"Yes," Abe's cold, bleak voice said behind him. "You will. The first time you cut a buck out of here or even look like you want to."

Francisco shot a dark look at Burrows and reached for the beaker of water, took it and held it out toward Jack. "You first," he said deliberately, to belittle Abe. Jack drank and handed the jug back, looking over at the older man when Francisco was drinking. For his own purpose — and also because he was inwardly excited and pleased at what he now knew — he smiled flintily at Abe.

"Listen, Mister, if you want to fight, I'll fight you any time, any way, and any place. If we're goin' to work here together, I'd rather get along. It's up to you."

"Bravo!" the *vaquero* said with strong approval. "Well? How will it be, then?"

Abe glowered a moment before he answered. "We'll see," was all he would say. "We'll see. Now, let's get to work. Ain't too many daylight hours left."

Jack's stupefaction lessened as the daylight drew out into a late twilight. It was revived though, when Francisco came lugging another sack of gold from the house. Jack squinted up at the Mexican. "None of my business, friend," he said, "but by golly, you fellers've got about all the gold in Mexico, haven't you?"

Abe walked up beside them with the prod-pole. He was looking coldly at Jack. "We got enough," he said. "You just do like you're supposed to do an' you won't go hungry."

Jack flushed and started to straighten out of his bent position beside the chute. Francisco swore very suddenly in Spanish, then in English. He was as fluent in one as the other and his black eyes shot fire at Abe. "I've had enough of this! There is no reason for this anger all the time. If you have trouble being pleasant, then keep the goddam mouth shut!"

That time it was Jack had to shove them away from each other. He did it with a wary eye on the Mexican's knife. "Rope it, dammit. Back up there, old man." He pushed Abe back with a powerful shove and stepped across between them, then swung back to Abe with a look of fierceness twisting his face. "The next time you do that, I'm going to stomp you into the ground."

Abe was chalky faced. The fist holding the prod-pole was white-knuckled with his anger, shaking a little. "I could kill you! Damn you for meddlin', I'll —"

"SHUT UP!" Jack roared it too loud. The crashing shout smashed against their eardrums with a stunning impact. They both stared at him when he whirled and went back by the chute fighting to regain his control.

The words spoken by Suzanne were already branded into his mind. Their repetition by her father made them like fire in his memory. He went to work with his back to them, slicing the little pocket in the next animal's undersides, poking in the gold grains and pinching closed the small opening. He didn't look around until he heard Abe's boots crunching back toward the end of the chute. Then Francisco came over and knelt by him, looking into his face.

"I think it will end now."

"Yeh," Jack said shortly. "Something will. What's the matter with the danged old fool?"

"Who knows? He is not a happy man. He had a son killed not long ago over in Arizona. He is bitter, perhaps."

"Why'n hell doesn't he go up and down the man who shot his son and quit taking it out on the world?"

Francisco's dark eyes were thoughtful and still for a moment, then he got up without a word and walked away. Jack found time to look around. He was over by Abe talking in a fast, clipped way. Abe's face was downcast and surly looking, but he was listening. When Jack turned back to his labour, the old man lifted his icy eyes and studied the tall, gaunt frame over by the chutes with a look as thoughtful as Francisco's had been. He walked away from the Mexican without a word.

Francisco came back by Jack. They worked together, hardly speaking, until darkness came, then Jack looked at the animals in the front corral. They were placidly eating hay and chewing their cuds. None showed any pain at all. He wagged his head at the strange sight and tried to notice the little bulges. He couldn't see them in the gloom and knew inwardly that in daylight

188

they would be just as hard to see from the ground, and from a horse's back there would be no chance at all.

"This is clever, no?"

"Damned clever. Damnedest thing I ever saw, Francisco. How much do you figure they carry — each one, I mean?"

"It differs but we figure between one ounce and two."

"More'n the cows are worth."

Francisco laughed. "Well, we don't want fat cattle. It is better this way. Lean cattle we can use many times. We feed them enough to keep them strong and hard, and we drive them a long enough way and often enough to keep them lean. It must always look like the men who are driving our cattle have just bought them skinny, in Mexico."

"Who thought this up, anyway? I never heard of anything like it."

"The man who thought it up is dead. His name was Lon Colley. He had a long time — many nights — to lie in the Yuma prison, thinking. He thought it all out and when he got back here again, we started doing it." Francisco smiled genially. "Oh, we have been smuggling for a long time, but this business we are in now, it has only been perfected for a year or so."

. . . Colley had thought it up in Yuma

189

prison, Jack marveled. If Amos Marlow knew what Jack knew, he'd be beside himself. There remained only a couple of loose ends yet to tie up.

Grimes. How did they get it to Grimes? That answer came out of the conversation he had heard the day before. Colley, Abe had said, used to run their pack outfit. He recalled the six bays and sets of harness in the Burrows' barn. Colley must have taken the gravel-gold down to Grimes' blacksmith shop with a pack train. Probably in the night. It wouldn't take him half an hour to unload and be on his way back to the Burrows place again.

"Damnedest thing I ever imagined," he said admiringly, aloud.

"But you don't know all of it, Jake," Francisco assured him. "When you do you'll like it even more."

Abe Burrows came over using the prodpole like a staff. "Let's go eat. I just saw Mark ride in."

They went to the house and washed sparingly from an earthen basin with water that was cool and alkali smelling, indicating where it had come from; then all three smugglers went about cooking supper. Mark rarely spoke to any of them and Jack had no occasion to speak, nor did he feel the inclination. His mind was chuck-full of startling revelations.

Five hundred head of cattle, each carrying from one to two ounces of pure gold in such a way that no one would ever suspect them of it, three, possibly four times a month. No wonder the Governor of the Territory had written to Malta over the amount of contraband being smuggled into the country! It amounted to enough money, if kept up just a little longer, to disrupt the gold basis of the Nation's currency.

He wasn't aware of Francisco looking at him. Nudging Mark with a tilt of his dark head he said, "His eyes, Mark; look at them." Mark looked and understood the Mexican's low tone and ironic smile. He, who had been in the business for over a year, had, in fact, seen it grow into the complex, highly successful ring it was now, was still appalled at the fantastic wealth each of them was piling up.

There was a change in Mark; he had achieved a deep-lying triumph over the man who had dominated him since he could remember, and that, even more than his private cache of gold, was personal wealth. He felt a kindliness toward Jack, who had helped him achieve it. He smiled at Francisco and turned back to the table.

"Come on, Peters," Abe called roughly. "At least you've earned your supper."

Jack ate with the rest of them. There was little said and when a conversation was instituted it was usually the affable Mexican who started it. Mark either answered in monosyllables or with as few words as he could. Abe rarely responded to whatever was said and Jack was in no mood to talk. He had just one thing on his mind: how he was going to get back to Malta alive.

He had no doubt about the Mexican's ability with his guns. More complex though, was the fact that Jack dared not even try to leave until the Burrowses took the 'loaded' cattle back over the line. So far they seemed to be completely lulled. He wanted them to stay that way. If anything made them wary now, everything he had sweated for — everything Amos Marlow counted on — would be undone. The safety of Abe and Mark Burrows couldn't have ever been better than it was right now, while they were in Mexico. They couldn't be extradited and they couldn't be arrested except by the Mexican constabulary corps, who laughing uproariously at the American attitude toward smuggling, helped themselves to bribes and turned their backs upon the American lawmen.

It was like riding a green-broke colt. He was momentarily safe — or felt that way, but at any second something might be said or done to throw suspicion on him. He was fully aware, too, that some strong tug-of-war between the father and the son was being played out in grim and savage silence, with his fate bound up in the result.

When they finished their meal Jack followed Francisco outside. The moon was nearly full. They made cigarettes and sat on a narrow bench beside the house. He looked up at the sky with its soft, purple light, and very methodically put it all together in his mind. Even the parts he had to fabricate from fragments of old conversations and circumstantial surmises completed the picture with very little discord.

It was almost unbelievable. Now, if only Amos had ferretted out the other end of the ring, between them they would have everything they needed.

"I am lonely out here."

He looked blankly at the *vaquero*. "Lonely? I reckon a man'd get that way. You stay here all the time?"

"*Sí,* someone must." The Mexican turned his soft eyes on Jack. He smiled. "You are full of questions, no?"

"Yes."

A careless shrug. "Ask them then. I can answer some. Others — not yet. I am a judge of men, too, like Burrows. On some of the things I will answer you."

"Where the devil does so much gold come from?"

"That is easy, Jake. From the Apaches. Where they get it I don't know." Francisco fished inside his shirt and brought out a great gold crucifix breathtakingly beautiful and fabulously wrought with pearls and silver and emeralds. "This, I have kept out. It must have come from some Mission — perhaps from an archbishop — who knows?" Francisco put the thing back inside his shirt again. "I myself could never own such a thing. It is beyond price, *amigo*."

"Yeh, I reckon the man's neck they took it off was beyond price too — if you think human life has value."

Francisco nodded agreeably. "Who would doubt that? But I only trade for it. I can't prevent what the Indians do. I don't even know where they will strike or when. I trade for their gold but that doesn't mean I approve of it all."

"What do you trade them?"

"Guns, bullets."

"I reckon you couldn't stop the 'Paches from killing and burning and raising hell.

194

But you sure help 'em do it when you give 'em that stuff."

"Ahh, no. If they didn't get it from me they'd get it from another trader. There are many on the border who cherish their trade. I do only what I can to live, Jake."

Jack laughed bitterly and softly. "You've sure got it all worked out in your mind so that it's not wrong, haven't you?"

"Are you concerned with right and wrong then, my friend?"

Jack met the dark gaze with one just as dark and steady. "I reckon not. It just seems to me — well — forget it. After all, if it wasn't for the damned Indians you wouldn't have the gold."

"Exactly."

"It's the damndest thing I ever heard of though. I can't get it all figured out even yet. I don't reckon I'd better ask where those fellers take the cattle."

"No, that I won't tell you, but I mentioned today to Abe that you might be handy on the trip some time. He has a man up in Arizona that he wants killed. This is the man who killed his son that I told you about. Well, I suggested to Abe that he hire you, a stranger up there, to ride with him and take care of this man."

. . . Ride to Arizona for the smugglers —

the men he was after — and get paid by them, as one of their ring, to kill himself! It was too fantastic. His brooding smile showed fleetingly, then he shook his head at the Mexican. "I'd rather not ride into Arizona for a long, long time. You understand."

"But of course. Only I didn't mean this trip. Maybe the next trip or the one after that. Who knows? Maybe Abe will do this killing himself. I would, if it was my son."

"Sure," Jack said. "Don't the gringos usually do their own killings?"

"Yes," Francisco said. "The old one is a tiger. He could kill his own mother I think, that old devil."

"He looks like it all right," Jack said evenly. "Has he ever killed anyone around here?"

"No, not down here, but up where they belong he is known as a bad man with a gun. I have heard many tales about him from the one that got killed up there — the man who thought this good scheme up."

"Yeah, well, who did —"

"Colley told me he knew the old man many years ago when he was a rider for cow outfits up there. He said the old man was known to have killed at least six men and some oldtimers told Colley that they could remember even more that he had shot to death. He is a formidable man with a gun, Jake. That's why I jumped between you two today. I don't know you but I do know the old man. Bad *hombre,* Jake. Bad *hombre.*"

Jack stomped out his cigarette. "Do you know of any one, yourself, that he's ever killed?" He looked at Francisco with a wry smile. "Those old buzzards have a way of building themselves up. I take what they say with a grain of salt, myself."

Francisco regarded the end of his cigarette with a little frown. He said slowly, "Yes, I know of one man he has killed since we have been in this business together." The brown eyes raised with a little shrug. "I don't think it was a good killing; still, it is a killing and that's what we are talking about, no?"

"Yes," Jack said, leaning far forward so the shadows would hide his face. "Who was it — a lawman?"

"No, it was like this, Jake. There is a ranch up near where the old man and his boy take our animals. There was a man who lived there and refused to move away, even for gold. Well, the trail we have always used ran across this man's ranch. You can understand we couldn't go driving back and forth in front of him, no?"

197

"Yes," Jack said in a tight way. "I understand. So the devil killed this rancher. Is that it?"

"Yes. What I said I didn't like, was that he did it with a formidable buffalo gun and from hiding." Francisco shuddered at the thought of the wound such a ball would make in a man's body.

"Yeah," Jack said solemnly, locking his fists together and picturing Will's laughter — the way he threw his head far back when he laughed. "Yeah, a thing like that'd make a hell of a mess of a man, wouldn't it?"

"It would indeed, Jake."

Jack raised his head after a long silence and swung it slowly, looking at the shadows for the thick, bearded figure. When he found it, he was alone on the platform by the corral, lounging up there smoking and gazing down at the cattle. Francisco couldn't see his face then, but if he could have he would have realised how much more appropriate his earlier remark would have been now.

"His eyes, *Señor;* look at them."

Chapter Five

Jack went out with the rest of them at dawn. They cut out all the crippled and old stock. It didn't take long but it was hard work and their horses were lathered before noon. After they had eaten and rested, Epifanio came in herding thirty-five replacements. These cattle were as nearly wild as they could be. Jack swore and sweated with Francisco as his riding companion, getting the spooky animals into the corrals.

Afterward, he and Mark were paired off at the chute, loading the animals with the contraband gold. Mark rarely spoke. He looked and acted sullen. Jack ignored him. The day was spent in arduous labour and in the evening they all pitched hay to the corraled cattle before going inside to eat. There, he noticed that Francisco and the brutal, pockmarked rider were involved in an argument. He could guess the reason for it from the unfriendly, murderous glares Epifanio shot his way from time to time. Epifanio wanted rid of him.

They ate stonily silent and Abe left them as he usually did, to be alone. Francisco and

Jack went back outside for an evening smoke.

Mark joined them after a while, to Jack's surprise. He squatted beside the bench and leaned back against the warm adobe wall. "Guess we'll head out in the morning," he said casually. Francisco sighed and smiled tiredly.

"This has been the hardest trip of all, so far."

"Wouldn't have been if Colt'd been here."

"No, you are right. I didn't mean just that, though. The Chief has been hard to live with this time. Harder than usual."

"He's got cause to be," Mark said. "Like he said, you boys don't have too much to fear down here. We have, over the line. Then there's the business of him and me doing all the work up north. There's a lot more to it than a feller'd think, sitting around down here."

Francesco spread his hands. "You know I can't go over the line, Mark. If I could, I'd go, you know that. Epifanio would be useless to you up there. That also is true."

"Oh, I reckon we can do like the old man says. Make a couple more trips by ourselves, but, dammit all, after that he's got to let us get some more help or he can do it all himself as far as I'm concerned."

The Mexican smiled wryly. "You are just talking, Mark. After all, we are making much money; much wealth."

"Dammit," Mark swore with crisp feeling. "I don't want all the money in the world. I want to spend it, not just die young making it."

"Well, why don't you take Jake back with you?"

Jack shook his head quickly. "I told you it wouldn't be safe, Francisco. What d'you think I was running for? Arizona's the last place in the world I want to go for a long time."

Mark scowled at the ground in front of him. "We don't go where folks are, Jake," he said, slowly, thoughtfully. "Anyway, if we seen riders coming you could hide out."

"I'd get caught," Jack said flatly.

"Not where we go. Not the way we go, either. Listen, Jake. It isn't hard. The cattle mostly know how to do it by themselves. They've been going over the same route for a year now. All we go along for is to shoot any that try and break away, strip out their pouches and be sure they aren't where anyone's likely to stumble onto them. Hell, if it wasn't for that we could push the danged things out on the range and turn 'em loose. They'd find their own way down here as soon as they got hungry."

"That doesn't mean *I'm* safe," Jack said grimly. "There's the law up there."

Mark was going to answer when Abe strolled over with Epifanio in tow. They both hunkered down in dour silence. Jack felt the hair along the nape of his neck rising. If ever two men looked thoroughly murderous, the black-eyed *vaquero* and the bearded American did. Mark gazed at them for a moment then went back to his argument.

"Sure, there's law up there, Jake, but we've pretty well figured a way around them. We don't go anywhere near where they're likely to be."

But Jack shook his head adamantly. "Mark, all that has to happen is for one lawman to come ridin'. He'd spot me for sure. I'm like you. Money's no good to me if I can't spend it."

"You afraid o' the law?" Abe said harshly.

Jack shot him a long, unfriendly look. "I've got reason to be. Like I told them, Arizona right now's the last place I want to go."

"Maybe," Abe said coldly, "you wouldn't have a choice."

Jack grinned at him wolfishly. "You'd be a plumb damned fool if you took me up there right now. What'd you gain? Maybe the law's got my picture by now, even. It'd endanger your whole set-up. No, I don't think you're that dumb, Abe, and I know I'm sure not about to stick my head into no rope, out of choice."

Abe looked at Jack with a thoughtful glance. "Mark just told you we don't use trails."

"Don't make a damn," Jack said stubbornly. "It's too risky."

Abe fished out his knife and started whittling idly, frowning. Francisco shrugged. "Let him stay down here for a while then, Abe. You can ask around when you get back. Maybe Tommy can find out whether he's wanted badly enough to be dangerous to us."

Abe whittled, saying nothing, and Mark bent over his tobacco sack. Only Epifanio, with his cold, merciless black stare, looked at Jack. He was like a rattlesnake, the way his eyes rarely blinked and fixed themselves on something. Jack moved a little on the hard bench.

"You got any money?" Abe asked suddenly, still whittling.

Jack fished out some limp bills and held them out. "That's all."

Abe looked up at him that time. "Where's the loot you got off the stage?"

Jack was startled by the question. "Hid," he said succinctly, realising how dangerous Abe was, with his spells of deep silence.

Mark spoke around his cigarette, watching his father's knife slide up and down on the whittled stick. "How much does he get?"

Abe went on whittling. "Five hundred a trip," he said slowly.

"I'm not going to make the trip," Jack said stubbornly.

"In that case," Abe said, grinning viciously, "a hundred dollars for working down here."

▸ Francisco looked disgusted but he said nothing. Mark looked at his father with no relish. Only Epifanio, whose knowledge of English didn't include conversations like this one, looked steadily and imperturably at Jack. Damn gringo, his look said; we don't want you on the ranch.

Abe clicked his knife closed and rocked back on his heels, looking up at them. "All right," he said. "He may be right at that. Anyway, I want to do a little nosing around up north about him before we let him make a drive." The baleful glance swung to Francisco. "He's the same as a prisoner here, so we'll let it ride like that. You keep a watch on him until we get back, Francisco, then we'll talk about it some more. Keep an eye on Epifiano here; he don't like him any more'n I do."

They broke up shortly after that, but before they went trooping into the house to sleep, Francisco touched Jack's arm and stood back a little, wearing a thin, sardonic smile. "See how the old devil is, Jake? First, he didn' want you around at all, then he used you in the corral. Now, because you don't want to go north on the drive, he wants you to. Contrary, you gringos call it; contrary and as mean as a wolf. Epifanio is urging him to take you away. He can't make up his mind."

Jack nodded, smiling back at the Mexican. "Bad *hombre*," he said.

They went in and threw themselves down on their blankets. Jack had only his old dun-coloured coat but the night was warm and the adobe house was downright hot. Usually cool during the day, the adobes gathered warmth so slowly that they held the heat surprisingly well after nightfall.

He lay there thinking, mostly about Abe. The old smuggler wasn't hard to figure out or understand. He was just mean; wolf-mean and murderous. It wasn't distrust of Jack so much as it was a personal hatred that had come out of being defied and faced down. Because of that Abe Burrows would have liked to force Jack — supposedly against his will — to make the drive with them. Abe's hating blindness was the one thing that came very close to making it possible to Jack to get back to Malta. Epifanio's dislike only weighed the more against leaving him behind.

He had played his part well. He knew that, because, aside from Francisco, he could see that sullen Mark Burrows was coming around a little.

Whatever thoughts they might have had, that part of his acting had left them with no reason to suspect him. He smiled up at the dark ceiling with a gloomy look in his hazel eyes. The one thing he wanted more than anything else, right now, was also the one thing he dared not let the men around him think he wanted at all, even if he had to let them ride out of the yard without him.

But he had an idea on that, too. He had the idea all afternoon; ever since he had seen how wild the replacement cattle were. He had even put it into effect partly when he had been alone in the corral for a few minutes. It hadn't taken long and involved nothing more difficult than the breaking of three strands of wire where the faggot corral was closest to the gate.

There was one wire left intact. If it didn't work like he wanted it to, then he'd have to stay with Francisco and pray that Amos Marlow had gotten enough information, perhaps from Grimes, to catch the smugglers on their return trip. If it *did* work, he'd go back with the Americans and they'd force him to go, which was the way he wanted it to look, especially to Abe.

At dawn he was awakened by a rude shaking Mark Burrows was giving him. He rolled over and sat up, frowning. Young Burrows was angry-eyed and sleepy looking. "Come on, Jake. Get your damned horse. The cattle have broken out."

"The loaded ones?" he asked, with a leaping heart.

But Mark was already running for the door, letting off a curse with almost every stride. Outside it was growing lighter by the minute. He saw Francisco saddling furiously, his face set and white looking. Abe was swinging up as Jake ran by. "Hurry up," he said raspingly, then swung away with a vicious spurring of his mount. Jake roped his horse and flung leather on, but as fast as he was, he was still the last man to thunder out onto the range where Mark was waiting for him with a twisted, furious expression. He reined up beside the younger man. "What's it all about? What happened?"

"Hell," Mark said excitedly, "how would I know? All I can say is that Epifanio wakened me shouting the damned cattle'd busted out of the corral. The loaded ones, too. Come on, we'll have to work fast."

They rode fast, fanning out through the coolness, twisting and turning and throwing themselves headlong at the brush clumps where wicked-horned, wily old cows were standing like statues, hoping to be missed or overlooked. Jack worked like the rest of them. With sweat running into his eyes and his heart pounding.

The dust lifted sullenly, thickly, from the moistureless earth. Cows would jump out in front of them, throw their tails over their backs and break for the erosion ditches or thick patches of spiny brush, trying to escape. The older cows didn't give much trouble. They were scattered badly, which let Jack know they had broken out early in the night, but they didn't try quite as desperately to elude the riders as the replacement critters did. The latter were like antelope.

Profanity punctuated the hard slamming driving of horse's hooves all morning. Finally Jack came across Francisco staring furiously at a wily critter that had plunged as far as it could get, into a dense and thorny manzanita clump, and now stood there glaring her long-horned defiance. The Mexican threw up his hands in exasperation.

"You see, Jake? This is what comes from thinking always the same way."

"What do you mean?"

"I used to insist that we always keep up a night guard over the cows after they are loaded. Abe said it wasn't necessary. I didn't want to argue with the old goat. We stopped having night guards. We all do what he says — think like he does — and this is what happens."

Jack eyed the cow speculatively, then walked his horse around behind the brush clump, dismounted and flagged her with his hat. She took the challenge and came out bawling and throwing her head. The sun shone darkly off her deadly horns. Jack swung into the saddle and whirled his horse when she went past. He drove her then, and she went, in a bawling, slavering fury toward the ranch. Francisco joined in.

They teased her into the corral and Francisco sat staring glumly at the broken place. "There," he said accusingly. "Right by the gate where they would naturally bunch up." He struck the saddlehorn and glared at Abe and Mark who came in with a big gather.

"After this we have a night guard, always!"

Abe said nothing. He even avoided looking at the Mexican's face while he and Mark worked their catch inside. Jack dismounted and went about patching the break. His face was wooden but his eyes shone metallically while he wove the wires back into place and spliced them. He went over to his hard-breathing horse and reached for the stirrup. Seeing Mark watching him, he spoke as he sprang up.

"Did you count 'em?"

"Yeah, just finished. We're shy some, dammit."

"Well, let's go hunt 'em, they can't be too far off."

"Naw," Mark said, swinging in beside him and riding across the yard to the shade where the others were unsaddling. "We'd waste all day trying to find the cussed critters and then we probably wouldn't get 'em. Let 'em go." In his weariness he was offering comradeship to a fellow rider.

Jack dismounted and looked over the seat of his saddle at Mark. "With the gold in 'em! Somebody'll find 'em sure. We dassn't."

Abe handed his reins to Epifanio and looked over at them. "Sure we can," he said. "Francisco and Epifanio'll be down here. They got nothing more to do but hunt 'em up and fetch 'em back or shoot 'em." The venomous little eyes swung toward Francisco. "Ain't that right?"

The Mexican shrugged. His face was pale with anger and he didn't look up at Abe. "Between the three of us we'll get them. Only we should've had a night guard —"

"The two of you," Abe corrected him curtly. "Them damned replacements're too bronko for jus' Mark an' me to take up t' Malta. We'll have to take Jake with us."

That time Francisco's face came up swiftly. Jack was surprised at the raging anger in it. He was afraid the Mexican was going to make a stab for his belted gun. Mark must have thought it, too, because he swung swiftly toward the *vaquero* and his voice was low. "Easy now, easy." But Francisco was too infuriated at Abe's high-handedness to relax.

Jack moved a little so as to obscure the Mexican's view of Abe Burrows. He was watching the man's face closely. "All right, Francisco. Let it go. I'll go with 'em. Let's not have trouble now. Let's see what happens up north. If worst comes to worst I'll have to run for it and try to get back here."

Francisco gave a small, almost imperceptible shudder and straightened up fully. He looked away from Abe's steely, watchful glare and moved away from the group. As he went past Jake he looked briefly into his face. "I think you'll be safe enough from the law, Jake. It's *him* — the old devil — I'd watch."

Abe turned to speak and Mark moved swiftly. He put himself in front of his father with both hands on his hips and a strange, wild smile in his eyes. "Shut up! Don't open your mouth! You've done nothing but make trouble this trip."

He turned and started after the Mexican, no longer a boy scared of his father but a free, full-grown man. Jack and old Abe were left alone.

Jack relaxed and said very softly, "What's the matter with a feller like you, Abe? You're makin' it impossible for anyone to get along with you. No one's afraid of you but you're makin' it so's they won't want to ride with you. Slack off on it. I thought Francisco was going to kill you. Someday someone will, if you don't quit being so hard to live with."

Abe didn't move nor answer until the last echo was gone, then he jerked his head toward the house. "Go fetch your stuff and come back an' get a fresh horse. Tell Mark to come back too; we'll start out now."

Jack crossed the yard with the uneasiness in his mind that told him old Abe was glaring after him. His shoulder blades felt hopelessly exposed. Inside the house Francisco and Mark were talking. They both glanced at him when he came in, paused, then went on talking. The Mexican was still pale in the face. "I hope you're right, Mark. I hope so. If he comes back the next time like he is this time — I don't know."

"It's been no cinch for me, pal, and it won't be any better goin' back. I got to take more of it than you do. We'll see if he gets any different after this Fulton hombre's out of the way. I really figure that's what's making him like he is."

"I hope so," Francisco said again, then he smiled dazzlingly over at Jack. "Many thanks my friend. I think maybe you kept one of us from being hurt."

Jack shrugged dourly. "He says for us to come back and pick fresh horses. We're riding out with the cattle now."

Francisco nodded dully. "Maybe it is best. Epifanio will be glad. He don't like you, Jake. Let's go." He pointed toward a bundle. "That's food, Mark. Epifanio and I'll go as far as the water-hole with you."

"Good," Mark said, hefting the bundle with one hand. "Don't forget to kill those critters that're still loose, will you?"

"No need to worry."

They trooped back out into the yard and down to the horse corral. Epifanio, like a silent, brown wraith, had their animals already tied outside and saddled. The old man was already astride. He looked past them and didn't speak, not even after they had opened the gate and lined the animals out. He rode off a little by himself, an outcast, and none of the others made any effort to ride with him.

The day was breathlessly hot and the dust stung like pepper. The cattle kept them occupied only until they smelt the water-hole, and after that they couldn't have held them if they wanted to. They drifted along in the drag, spitting dust and breathing behind their hands, riding in a little group, the five of them.

At the water-hole Francisco caught Jack aside and looked into his brooding face. "Watch him, Jake," he said. "I meant it back there when I told you that. He's worse than I've ever seen him." He swept back his Charro jacket and held out Jack's pistol, butt-first. "You can always rely on this."

Jack took the gun gratefully but he frowned as he holstered it. "He won't like havin' me armed."

"To hell with him," Francisco said pleasantly. "Come, that's your carbine in my saddleboot."

Jack took the carbine too, then, when they were ready to start the drive and the cattle were logy with water, he saw Mark's gaze on his holstered six-gun.

"You mind?" he asked.

Mark cast an unconscious little glance at his father who was lining out the pointers, and shrugged. "*I* don't," he said. "The old man might. Where'd you get 'em; from Francisco?"

"Yeah."

Mark reined over beside him. "Well, don't say anything if the old cuss doesn't. It might be all right."

They swung once, when a long, undulating roll of land lifted them above the countryside a little, and they waved to the small figures close together back down by the water-hole. After that they didn't talk much. Just smoked and watched the cattle string out. Once, a bunch-quitter — one of the wild replacement critters — made a break for it. Like three avenging fates all three riders swooped down on her, boxed her in and forced her back again. That put them all together and they rode that way for several awkward miles. To test Abe's mood, Jack made a cigarette and offered him the sack. He got a refusal but it wasn't with one of the old man's customary nasty remarks.

He tendered the sack to Mark, who took it and bent to the work of making a cigarette.

"See that lift 'way off up ahead?" Abe said gruffly. Jack nodded. It was the same rib of land he'd first spotted them from on the way down to Mexico. Much had happened since then. It was almost unbelievable. "Yeah."

"That's the route we take," Abe said, then closed his mouth after the words like he'd said twice as much as he'd meant to.

Mark smoked and had a sardonic look in his eyes. Jack exhaled and winked at Mark, very solemnly and gravely. The sullen younger man's face split in a tight, grudging smile. Soon after that Abe spurred up toward one side of the herd where several of the replacement critters were weaving in and out, unable to make up their minds whether to risk breaking out of the herd or not. Mark watched his father ride up and spurt toward the recalcitrants, frightening them back into place, and he shook his head and spat over the side of his saddle.

"Damned old cuss," he said. That and no more. Jack wisely said nothing, but he understood: Mark was free of his father's domination.

The trail back was seemingly endless to Jack. He was armed. More than that, he had a reasonable scope of range that neither of the two men begrudged him. With Abe there was little enough contact. Jack avoided the older man except when he couldn't do so without appearing obvious. With Mark he came, in time, to ride and talk.

He sought this diversion gladly in order to dull the anxiety within him. Also, he was curious about the younger man. Mark was as hard as nails. There was much of his father in him. But there were also some streaks he hadn't gotten from Old Abe. Mark had a sullenness that wasn't hard to understand, but he also had a deep torment of some kind within him that made him disagreeable and uncommunicative at times. Almost as though he hated people; not especially his father or Jack, but just people; any and all of them.

In the late afternoon, Jack rode far ahead once, and sat for a long time on a land-swell, looking. He was hoping to see a posse somewhere in the distance but he didn't. He rode back glumly and passed the old man. Abe shot him a sardonic glance then looked away. Mark was off to one side of the drag when he came down beside him, turned his horse and rode stirrup with him.

"You sure worry a lot about posses," Mark said.

Jack frowned at his horse's ears. "It's bad enough to be wanted up here," he answered Mark, "but it's a whale of a lot worse to be riding back up into this country with — what we've got."

Mark snorted and grinned. "I've done this so many times now I don't even get leary when a rider comes by."

"Do they? Do you see riders?"

"Once in a long time. We're crossin' range that's shared by some pretty big oufits." He looked with a bored glance at the dusty, heaving backs of the herd. "Look at 'em." He shook his head and spat. "I can't even tell it myself, when they're walking along like that. You'll see, Jake. Sometimes when we go to take it out you can hardly find the pouch 'thout running your hand over 'em. They're pretty danged hairy under there."

Jack agreed mentally. "I hope we don't run into anyone this trip."

"Don't worry. If we do they won't know anything."

"No?" Jack said. "Not on the cattle, or you and Abe — but I'm a little different, Mark. I'd just as soon stay low for a while."

"Well, when we get back I'll leave you and the old man to do the unloading while I get some sleep. When you've got it all out I'll take it down to the smelter."

"Smelter?"

"Yeah. There's a feller in Malta who burns the stuff in forges. This feller, Colley, set his old riding pardner up in a blacksmithing shop in Malta. He melts the gold down and mixes forge-clinkers in with it and dumps it."

"What d'you mean, dumps it?"

"Takes it out on the range and just chucks it like it's regular old forge ash. The fellers who buy it have another forge over near Florence. They pick it up at the dump, take it to their place, heat it again, take out the clinkers, make it into little bars and sell it to some fellers from Dodge City, over in Kansas."

"I'll be damned. All this was one man's idea?"

"Yeah, Lon Colley was plenty smart." Mark sighed. "A whelp named Fulton was in our way. Lon tried to scare him out. He didn't tell the old man he was going over to see this Fulton and it was raining like the devil. Just after this Fulton killed my brother the old man came back from Malta raising hell. The rain'd hide his tracks for him, he thought, so he rode over to drygulch this Fulton feller and shot Lon by mistake. We didn't know about it for a few days, then I heard about it in town and damn near passed out."

"So Fulton's still alive."

"Not for long, Jake. Not for long. I haven't said anything to the old man, but if he don't fix Fulton this trip I'm goin' to."

"How'd he kill your brother?"

"Colt come up from Mexico because Lon Colley and the old man couldn't agree on how to get rid of Fulton. Lon didn't want to drygulch him and the old man did, but seeing Lon'd lambaste him sure if he did it himself he brought Colt up to do the job. And Fulton foxed him. There was a dummy made up to look like Fulton. Colt shot and about a second later Fulton shot too. He killed Colt."

"So now it's just you and the old man."

"No," Mark said musingly, drawn out more by Jack's interest. "No, I've got a sister. She stays at the ranch. Sometimes she goes up on the ridge and keeps watch for us when we're unloading the cattle."

"What's her cut, Mark?"

"Cut? Hell, she don't get any cut. Fact is, Jake, she thinks we buy this gold on the States side of the border and hide it like this so's we won't get robbed fetching it home."

"She's pretty gullible, then," Jack said, looking straight ahead at the lowering shadows and the richer, grassier country coming toward them as the reaches of the Mexican desert fell back and away.

"Aw, you know how girls are, Jake. Suzanne's smart enough about some things. She's a whale of a good cook and she's a fair rider and stuff like that. Maybe she just doesn't know men too well." Mark shrugged. "Anyway, the old man told her that and she never chirped about it afterward because he said for never to breathe a word about it or we might all get killed in our sleep some night. Damn, it'd make you laugh the way she stands on a point o' rock above the ranch when we're unloading, keeping watch. Like an Indian, almost."

"Yeah, it'd be funny all right, I can see that."

He left Mark shortly after their talk and rode on ahead again. It was almost too dark to see a posse now if one was coming, but he wanted to ride up ahead where the dust and smell of cattle were out of the air. Wanted to just ride a little while by himself. His hate for Abe was like white-hot metal. One son ordered to murder a man and killed on the job; the other son warped, almost beyond saving; the daughter a dupe . . .

He rode as a sort of point rider for over an hour, then he heard a horse loping behind him and turned to find Mark reining up. "The old man says we've got to let 'em lie over for a couple of hours, Jake."

"Sure. Night camp?"

"No, when we drive we go right on through. No night camps, but he says we didn't weed out all the sore-legged ones." Mark swung back toward the slowing herd, looking dourly at it. "He's madder'n a caught skunk, too."

"Why?"

"Well, you see, the worst part of the drive is ahead of us about five miles. It's a big foothill patch of lava rock. If they're sore-footed now, some of 'em, what'll they be when we get into the hard-rock country?"

Jack said nothing but followed Mark down to where Abe, his beard bristling and his venomous eyes hot and dry with consuming wrath, awaited them. The cattle, no longer being pushed, were either grazing or bedding down. Abe flung out a thick, stubby arm. "There, you cow-savvy cut-out men! Look at that old girl, dammit, she can hardly stand up."

"It's only one," Jack said, in spite of the warning look Mark shot at him.

"One?" Abe stormed, his voice getting a throbbing overtone to it. "One? Damn you, look there; there's another one. And back yonder, next to the old crumpled horn girl. That steer's packed more gold than you'll ever see. He's another one. You were supposed to cut out the sore-foots!"

"How's the country ahead?" Jack asked, looking at the animals with a little ripple of uneasiness within him.

"It's hell from the end of this grass on."

"Trees?"

"Yeh," Abe spat out grudgingly.

Jack shrugged. "If we can get 'em to the trees and under some cover the worst that'll happen is that we'll have to shoot a few or leave one of us to fetch 'em along slower."

Abe grunted, fished up a plug of chewing tobacco and after worrying off a corner of it, tongued it up into his cheek and spat lustily. "*If* we get 'em to the foothills and the trees — *if*." He swung to Mark. "How'd you come to miss 'em, boy?"

Mark didn't answer. He seemed to be debating a short, truthful answer by the look on his face, but he never said it. The old man swore a little and swung down with a grunt. "Well, at least we can eat, too, for a change."

They ate with the smell and sounds of cattle around them. Once, Mark rode off ahead of the herd to see if any of the older critters were hastening home ahead of the others. A few were, but they were doing it in a slow, grazing way. He brought them back easily and came back to where Jack and Abe were squatting in thick, gloomy silence.

Jack was busy with his thoughts. He had Will's killer within arm's reach of him and knew it — and could do nothing about it. He also knew that soon now, before dawn, he'd have to manage to get away from Abe and Mark and ride like the devil for Malta. He had to work that so as to arouse no suspicion among the smugglers. Either that, or do it on a dead run and return with Amos and a posse before either Abe or Mark grew suspicious. The thoughts were chasing themselves around inside his head when Mark dropped down with a grunt and folded up the cloth with the food in it.

"We'd best be moving," he said. "Be better to lose a few in the trees than hang around out on the range after sunup."

Abe got up agreeing in a blisteringly profane way. He caught his horse, mounted it, and sat watching the two younger men. "Jake," he said, "ride with me for a spell."

Jack did. They hoo-rawed the cattle to their feet and lined them out, using their quirts on the indignant and reluctant ones until the whole herd was ambling along again. Then Abe spat forcefully and reined over beside Jack.

"Francisco give you back your guns?"

"Yeah."

Abe rode a hundred feet before he spoke again. "You ever notch a gun?"

"No. What the hell for?"

"For dead men — what else?"

"That's for greenhorns," Jack said scornfully. "Greenhorns and those old duffers who used to keep a coup-stick for every Indian they killed."

Abe's glance was like polished granite. "Well, some o' those old fellers run up a pretty good score. How are you on the killin'?"

"I'm still alive," Jack said shortly, beginning to suspect what was coming, and contemptuous of this old killer for not doing his own dirty work. He had already come to suspect Abe's deadliness was merely facade. The remnants of courage from his early days were insufficient when it came to hunting down Jack Fulton, who had bested him twice.

After that they rode in a depth of silence for a long time. Almost until Mark came back to tell them the trees were visible up ahead. Then he said, "You're makin' five hundred dollars on this drive. I'll make it an even thousand if you'll kill a man for me and fetch his guns and wallet to me at the ranch."

Jack had an almost instantaneous thought. "Where is he?"

"First," Abe said gruffly, "tell me if you'll do it."

"Sure. Give me the five hundred right now and tell me where he is, and if he isn't in the middle of a town I'll do it right now — tonight, before it gets light."

Abe nodded his head swiftly because he saw Mark coming toward them. "Done. It's a trade. Now keep your mouth shut around Mark about this. I'll see you later." He gigged his horse and went loping by Mark, who threw him a frown and called out.

"Hold it; the lava's up ahead. You want to angle 'em along the foothill and favour the sore ones?"

"No," the old man called back bluntly. "I'll point 'em now and we'll take 'em right up and around like we always do." He kept on his way.

Jack came abreast of Mark and saw the younger man's dark look. "What's the matter?"

"The damned old devil. He wouldn't favour a sore-footed critter but he'd raise the devil with us for missin' five or six out of five hundred. Makes me sicker'n hell, sometimes. Well — you see that dark skyline up ahead of us? That's hard-rock country, Jake. Hold 'em like they're goin'. For the old girls there won't be any steerin' needed. We'll just sort of hang back down here in case the limping ones or the spooky newcomers decide to make trouble."

They rode like that until the softly made complaints from some of the sore cattle told them that most of the herd was in the rocks, then the old man appeared loping through the moonlight toward them. He held up a balled-up fist toward Mark and motioned with it. "You take the point now, Mark," he said, and swung in close to Jack, watching Mark lope ahead with an angry shake of his head.

"Here." He opened his fist. There was a thick wad of crumpled old bills in it. "Count it. Five hundred even."

Jack didn't count it at all. He shoved the money into a pants pocket and turned fully to face Abe. "Where is he and who is he?"

"Name's Fulton." The old man turned a little in his saddle and pointed south of the uplands they were riding west over. "Down there, dang near due south of where we are now, there's a big soddy. He lives in there."

Jack looked out over the still, beautiful night with an unpleasant smile around his mouth. "Any other soddies I might mistake for his, down there?"

"None. He's got the only place for seven miles in any direction of our place."

Jack turned back to face Abe. His hazel eyes were as blank as stone. "Where do I go after I down him?"

"See where the trees up ahead dip down on the skyline?"

"Yeah."

"Ride over there and you'll find a big valley the other side of the cliff up there. That's our place down in the valley. If you can't trail the cattle to the down-trail, shoot a couple of times and one of us'll come and guide you down."

"All right," Jack said. "Is this the same feller that shot your other son?"

"Yeh."

"He's pretty coyote, isn't he?"

"You gettin' scairt?" Abe asked tauntingly.

Jack stared into the venomous old eyes and shook his head. "No, I'm not. But I figure this Fulton's got your number. If *you* weren't afraid of him, you'd do this job yourself." He gleaned a measure of grim triumph from the look that splashed down over the old man's face, then he reined off the trail and struck out due south, into the warm moonglow and away from the hard-rock country.

When he was down on the grassy plain again, he lifted his mount into a mile eating lope and swept down the night like a wild spirit. He saw his soddy from a distance and roared on past holding a course for Malta. He didn't draw rein until several little orange splashes of light showed weakly against the pale night, then he let the horse walk. The big animal was breathing hard. He had covered a lot of miles.

Malta was dead except for one drowsy, off-key piano that made dismal sounds from a saloon. The roadway was deserted. He rode down it to the sheriff's office, flung off, tied up and kicked open the door and stared into the startled face of a half-awake deputy sheriff. The man got no chance to speak. "Where's Amos?"

"Amos?"

"Yes, dammit. Amos Marlow, the sheriff. Where is he?"

"Why — a-bed I reckon." The deputy began to get out of his chair.

"Show me where he lives."

"I can't leave here. Sheriff's orders. I got —" The man's eyes dropped to the single sinister eyesocket of Jack's pistol. He seemed to suck in his belly a little.

"Come on, *hombre,* and move fast. I'm in a hurry."

The deputy moved fast, too. He went out of the office and scurried south to the first side street, ducked down it and almost trotted to the third house on the north side of the road. Jack's long legs and probing gun-barrel actuated him beyond his normal method of walking. "This here's the house. He'll be a-bed. He won't like —"

"Knock on the door. No, dammit — like this!" The door quivered drunkenly under the powerful impact of Jack's fist. They waited. The deputy looked more astonished than indignant. When Amos opened the door he had a pistol in his fist and a drugged look in the face.

"Who the — ? Jack! Lord, boy —"

"Get a posse, Amos."

The sheriff's seamed face screwed up into an excited stare. "You got 'em?"

"No, but I know how they do it and they're soon going to be back at their ranch with the cattle we brought from Mexico."

"We?"

"Dammit, Amos, I can explain any time. Right now you got to get a posse and move fast. Come on, will you!"

"Sure, sure." The sheriff turned swiftly toward his slack-mouthed deputy. "Dutch, run fetch Lewt and you two boys round up a posse." He looked back at Jack. "How many do we need?"

"I don't know. Five or six ought to be enough to seal 'em off in their valley."

"Dutch," the sheriff said, "get ten or twelve men and run, boy. I'll meet you at the office. Horses and guns all round. Run, dammit!"

The deputy ran. Amos watched him scurry at high speed down the walk toward the heart of town. He jerked his head toward the parlour behind him. "Come on in while I get my britches."

Jack shook his head. "I'll wait for you down at the office."

"No, consarn it, come on in. I got a lot to tell you."

Jack entered the dark house and stood in the middle of a musty smelling room. Hurrying to dress himself, the sheriff shouted out mutedly from some farther away room, grunting as he did so.

"I got Tommy in jail. Night after you disappeared some men came to town from the Capitol. The Governor sent 'em. I got rid of 'em by sending 'em over by Florence to nab those boys over there who were melting the stuff down and taking out the clinkers. But that sort of forced my hand too, for I knew then Tommy'd hear what was happenin' and maybe fly the coop.

"I locked him up and told him all I knew. He didn't say a cussed word until the Governor's men came back with their story. You'd never believe it, Jack, but by God those fellers was re-selling that gold as far away as Kansas City."

"What'd Grimes say to that?" Jack called out.

"Oh, he told the whole story then, only we couldn't get him to say a cussed word about how the gold got to his forge."

"Come on, doggone it, sheriff. I'll tell you the rest of it while we're riding."

Amos was askew from boots to hat, but his eyes shone with a look of excitement they hadn't held in twenty years. He smiled quickly. "Let's go."

They found seven men at the office and mounted up without waiting. Five more showed up in a lather as the possemen were loping north out of Malta. Lanterns sputtered and the town came drowsily, bewilderedly to life. By the time tousled heads peered out windows, the thunder of racing horses was a small echo in the moon splashed distance.

Jack paced his horse's gait to the slower gallop of Amos' animal. He told the sheriff all he knew in quick bursts of words. "That's all of it, sheriff. Fit it in with what you know and you'll have the doggondest scheme a man ever cooked up in one head."

Amos rode with his eyes nearly closed, piecing the story together. He was as staggered by it as Jack had been. He didn't say a word until Jack reached over and touched his arm, then he turned with raised eyebrows. "More? I never dreamt o' such a thing, Jack. Never in my life."

"No; that's all. Did the Governor's men round up those smelters over by Florence and the men they sold to, from Kansas?"

"Yup. The whole herd of 'em's in jail in Florence."

"How's Suzanne?"

Amos was turning away. His head swung back with a start. "Her? Oh, she's all right. You know what, Jack. That cussed gal hasn't said two words since you left her with me. Not two danged words. The Governor's men did everything but get down on their prayer-bones, and she just sat there like a wooden Indian. I never saw the beat of her."

"She's all right though?"

"If a danged block of stone is all right, why then I'd say she's just fine."

"She didn't mention me?"

Amos wagged his head. "She didn't mention nothing; not a cussed word. Miz Marlow went over and talked to her twice.

The last time she put her head on my wife's shoulder and cried like her heart was going to plumb wash away, but d'you know, Jack, she still wouldn't talk. I never saw one quite like that young lady."

"She's as pretty as a picture, isn't she, sheriff."

Amos slammed his mouth closed like a steel trap. His eyes were speculative the way they studied the gaunt, grey face of the man beside him. He didn't answer.

Jack led them up past the distant silhouette of Will's soddy. He skirted the trees and stopped them once to listen. A long way off, far ahead of them, westward and northward up in the trees, they heard a cow bawl. Jack smiled bleakly at Amos and slacked off his reins. They rode slower now, strung out and hunched up against the faint touch of cold that crept down around them. Jack beckoned Amos closer and jerked his head back at the shadowy riders. "Bunch 'em up, Amos. I don't think there's any danger because there's just the two of them, but let's ride close anyway."

Amos went down the line urging the possemen to stay together. By the time he got back up where Jack was, they were moving through the forest. Jack stopped when the men were grumblingly cursing their way among the trees. He dismounted, watched the others follow his example then, with Amos beside him, eyes alight, he led them to the path downward and stopped.

"Amos, as far as I know this is the only way down. They'll hear us sure as the devil. Now I've got an idea. I'll go down afoot — you lead my horse down. Once I'm down there I can stir the cattle up so's they'll bawl and move around a lot. That'll make enough noise to shield you boys. After you get down there, surround the house. Let the damned cattle go; we'll get them later. Make your surround good, too. If either one of them gets away we'll have wasted a lot of work. All right?"

"All right," Amos said shortly. "Gimme the reins."

Jack shed his spurs and hung them on his rear rigging D. He took his carbine and started down the path. The night made the cattle below him resemble small black spots, like balls, that rolled as they grazed. He thought dourly that they wouldn't — just this once — be making any noise. He'd have welcomed a lot of bawling but they were eating and silent — the only time since he'd first seen them.

He made it to the bottom of the trail and strode with his long, swinging steps toward the nearest animals. At sight of a man afoot they threw up their heads and snorted at him. He hurried, almost trotted, until he had the critters milling, their restlessness a contagion that spread. Then the bawling started, and with it, the animals began to move uneasily in the big meadow. He worried them constantly, never allowing them to become accustomed to his being among them. He also kept a wary eye on the house — and remembered in one startled moment that the ransacking he'd given the place would make both Abe and Mark chary. . . . And with Suzanne gone!

It was too late to warn Amos. He saw a horseman riding toward him leading a horse. The other riders were lost in the shadows of the moonlit valley. He went forward swiftly and swung up. "Amos, I forgot to warn you. They'll be suspicious. I ransacked the cabin before I went south after them."

Amos shrugged. "Won't make no difference, Jack. I've used these boys before. It'll take one hell of a gunman to down any of them, as well as they like living. Come on."

Jack rode toward the cabin watching the light coming out of it. He and the sheriff were almost within pistol range when Mark's thick silhouette showed up in the doorway. The bawling was subsiding a little. Jack reined up, watching. Amos' carbine made a slithering sound as it came out of the saddleboot.

"Hold it, Amos. Let's try it the other way first."

"Sure," the sheriff said blandly, "I always do. Holler once for them to toss down their guns then shoot. The only way, Jack; you got to give 'em a chance. That's the law."

Jack reached over angrily and knocked the carbine aside. "Let me do it, Amos."

The sheriff never got a chance to speak. A blast of rolling gunfire split the night wide apart. It came from the rear of the cabin and a bull-bass roar followed in its wake. Jack had no trouble recognising Abe's voice.

"Mark! Mark! The damned place's surrounded!"

Mark leapt back inside and slammed the cabin's front door. Jack swore sulphurously and dismounted two steps behind Amos, who was already kneeling, his carbine up again. There were no targets and even while Jack watched, the light inside was suddenly quenched. Only the moonlight remained.

Jack knelt holding his carbine loosely, scowling toward the cabin. Up to now the moonlight had been in their favour; now it was the other way around. He swore again and left Amos behind as he stalked forward. The sheriff watched him walking down the night toward the cabin. He lowered his carbine and squinted in a puzzled way, then he grunted to his feet and waited to see what Jack was going to do.

A deep stillness filled the valley that was broken only by distant cattle lowing. The cabin loomed ominously square, dark and forbidding. Close enough to see good, Jack veered off toward the old barn to give himself a solid background. A shot crashed outward from the back of the cabin and a man's shrill cursing indicated one of the possemen's carelessness in exposing himself. Jack knelt with a corner of the old barn protecting him.

"Mark?"

There was no answer. Jack tried again and the night seemed to listen. The eeriness of many eyes probing for a target was heightened by Jack's call. Mark must have heard but he didn't call back.

"Mark? Come out of there. The cabin's surrounded. They're out to get you, boy, and they will."

"Is that you, Jake?" Mark's tone was riddled with quick-firing fury, and doubt.

"Yeah, it's me, Mark. Come on —"

"You dirty, rotten —"

Jack let it rise to the crescendo of Mark's fury without answering, then, when the tempest had spent itself and the hush settled down again, he tried once more. There was a heaviness in him that showed in the brooding background of his eyes. "Listen, Mark, what you think of me doesn't matter, but you'd better come out of there. The odds are too big, boy, and you know your heart wasn't in the smuggling game anyhow. Why sweat it out?"

Mark revealed his position with a vicious shot that spanked into the area where Jack knelt. The tall gaunt man didn't flinch. He was still down on one knee watching the cabin when someone let out a roar of triumph that was quickly taken up by others. Jack saw the reason without understanding any of the bedlam of excited, exulting voices, that grew each moment until the night was alive with men's cries. Someone had gotten close enough to the rear of the cabin during Jack's and Mark's calls, to fire the place. Dry and bleached as the old cabin was, it fell ready prey to the licking spirals of flame.

Jack leaped up with a curse. A fusillade of gunfire broke out and kept him in the lee of the barn until it subsided. By then the flames were red and crackling. It was no longer possible to save the cabin. He saw men flitting through the shifting shadows, retreating from the heat and taking cover from the illumination. They hurried further into the forest that lay a hundred feet or so from the rear of the burning house.

"Jack? Where the hell are you? Jack?"

He heard the call and placed the voice. So did one of the men in the house. A long dagger of flame shot out from a small window opening. Jack shot his carbine from the hip. The bullet slashed out a long, pale splinter from the window-jam. He levered his carbine again and squinted through the hectic pattern of shifting firelight for the man who had called to him. When he saw him, he saw also that he was down in the churned grass.

The way to the wounded man was across the open ground before the cabin. He listened to the wild noise the growing fire was making and the desperate shooting of the besieged men and waited for a lull. None came. It was as though Mark and old Abe had determined to sell their lives dearly and go down with the cabin. He made a bitter face and waited until the sound of the gunfire seemed to shift toward the west wall, then he ducked low and ran to the wounded man.

No shot came. He threw himself flat and rolled the man over, grasped him by one arm and began to worm back out of the red, twisting flame-light that showed them both so glaringly.

"Where you hit?"

"In the hip, dammit."

Until the man spoke Jack hadn't paid any attention to his face. Now he flashed him a sharp look. "Amos! Was that you hollering at me?"

"Yeh. Take it easy, will you! This thing hurts."

Jack couldn't do it any differently than he was doing it. He had to stay low and work his burden backwards, hoping he'd be out of range or at least out of the light, before one of the embattled men in the cabin noticed him. "It'll hurt a lot worse if they see us. Crawl a little, Amos."

They slithered a long way, until the flame-glow was soft and obscure over them, then Jack let go of the older man's arm and sat up. He put his carbine aside and rolled the sheriff over roughly. "Hold still a minute." The wound was of the flesh. No bones had been hit at all. He leaned back and looked at the sweat-shiny, drawn face of the lawman. "You'll live, Amos. Plug those holes with pieces of your shirt-tail or something. I'm going back. You stay out here and lie still. When I get a chance I'll send a couple of the boys back for you."

"Wait —"

Jack was standing, reaching for his carbine when it came; a long, shrill, piercing scream such as an Indian would make when he knew this would be his last charge into the face of his enemies. Jack froze where he was. The scream drowned out Marlow's voice and much of the splattering gunfire back at the cabin. Jack's upper lip grew suddenly beaded with sweat. He gripped the carbine tightly and raised up to his full, long height.

The spectacle was one of terrible drama. The cabin was fully backgrounded in flame, blood red and wrenching upwards in tortured spirals that illuminated the whole wide valley now. The interior of the place was sullen scarlet. He could see it through the lopsided door that hung aslant and the one broken window in the front of the cabin.

Then he saw them running. Neither of them had a carbine but each had a vomiting six-gun that roared its deeper thunder over the smashing fire of the posse-men's guns. It was like being unseen and watching something you wanted to prevent and couldn't;

like being a part of another world, some way. A witness to horror that sickened you and you were hopelessly unable to do anything about.

He wasn't conscious of running toward the fleeing desperadoes until a gun went off with a shattering blast behind him. He stopped, stunned by the closeness of the explosion, his head ringing, and watched the figure in the lead stop as though he had run into a mighty and visible fist. The head went down, the legs bent a little, the man collapsed slowly, stubbornly, and Jack turned in his tracks. Amos was lying prone behind his carbine. A tendril of smoke trickled upwards in the moonlight, darker, dirtier looking than the detached coolness of the night.

He didn't turn back until men were shouting, and when he did he saw two grotesque lumps of darkness on the ground, the red flames licking over them with their dazzling brilliance. He dropped his carbine and went forward with the long, springing stride he had. The heat struck at him with a tangible force, recoiled off his face and hit lower, across his chest. He hurried, seeing other shadowy figures emerging from the brush and trees and from over by the old barn. He ignored them all until he was close enough to gaze at the two downed men. Abe was dead. He saw that in one glance. He had caught Amos' shot high in the brisket, plumb centre. He hadn't lasted five seconds — not three seconds — after the slug had smashed into him.

The firelight made his face a strange and unreal mask of red. He left Abe and bent over Mark. The younger man's eyes were closed and his mouth was ashen, quivering. He grasped Mark's shoulder and lifted him, threw him over his shoulder like a sack of meal and turned away. There were hurrying men around him, all talking at once, eyes wild and glistening in the red glare. He towered above them with his gaunt height. "Some of you carry the dead man out a ways. The rest of you surround the cabin and beat out the sparks. Don't let that fire spread to the barn or the forest!"

He pushed through them without graciousness and stalked back out where Amos lay. Mark's limp body was heavy. The heat beat against Jack's back with blistering fury. When he saw the sheriff sitting up working over the gory wound in his flesh, he stopped and eased Mark down and got down on both knees beside him. Amos peered from under a light-shielding hand at the body. "That's the young 'un," he said. "I particular wanted the old man, damn his lights."

"You got him," Jack said bleakly.

Amos returned his frosty look with one just as cold. "Good," he said emphatically. "I seen him just before he shot me." Amos dropped his glance to Mark. "Is he dead?"

Jack didn't answer. He searched for blood and found it high on Mark's head where the hair and scalp were torn and matted under a huge and growing swelling. He probed it and found the bone beneath hard and un-giving. He reared back on his heels and shook his head, looking glumly at the quiver-ing, bluish face of the wounded man. "No, he isn't dead. Someone aimed for a head shot and came as close as you can come without killing. He's out like a lantern though."

"Skull crushed?"

Another head shake. "No, doesn't feel like it. Just put him out is all, from the looks of it."

"Then," Amos said very practically, "you'd best take his belt and make his arms fast behind his back."

But Jack didn't do it. Mark was unarmed and unconscious. Jack stood up and looked over at the cabin. It was almost gone. Only four walls stood and while he watched one of those fell into the white-hot cauldron that had been the interior. He glanced back at Amos. "You watch him, sheriff. He won't be round for a long time, but you watch him just the same."

"What're you up to?"

"I'm going to send back to Malta for a buggy and the sawbones. Neither you nor the kid'll be able to ride astride." He walked back toward the cabin. Sweaty-faced men were using sacks and saddle-blankets and even old pieces of canvas to control the sparks. Jack took two of them aside from a place where the danger was the least. "You boys ride for town and fetch back the doctor and a buggy that'll haul Amos and young Burrows."

"They wounded or dead?" a tall, grey-eyed man asked.

"Wounded."

"Well," the posseman said, throwing down his sack. "Danged good thing there was lots of cover, wasn't it?"

"Yeah. Get your horses and ride hard, boys. I'd like to have 'em both out of here before the sun gets up."

The men left in a trot. Jack walked around the cabin. The flames were dying for lack of new fuel, but they were whiter than ever and a cherry-pinkness lay in the heart of them where the rubble was the thickest. The cabin was gone. There was just a pile of wreckage where it had been. The possemen trooped over to where Jack was and stood looking back at the ruin in silence. Jack twisted a little and looked into their faces. "All here?"

"Yeah, I reckon," a short, burly man said. He sounded very tired.

"Let's go over where the sheriff is, then."

They obeyed, dragging their blankets and sacks and old pieces of canvas. Amos was grimly in good spirits. One of the men produced a little pouch of coffee beans. The others took heart from this and scattered out to get water, stones, pitch-sticks and anything they could find to boil and drink the brew with. Time didn't drag as much as Jack had thought it would. They did what they could for Mark Burrows, and Amos had already done as much for himself as anyone except a medical man could do.

They sat there in the warm, glowing night like lumps of misshapen clay dumped at random in a sort of careless circle. They smoked and drank coffee and talked desultorily about the fight. An hour or so later, when reaction set in, several men lay back and snored up at the clear, milky night.

Just before dawn the buggy came. With it were five more riders. Jack stood aside while the rushing tide of conversation poured out on both sides. He saw a man leading their horses up, went and claimed his, mounted it and struck out for the path that led up out of the valley. He rode alone, forgotten by the others until the sheriff tried to find him, and by then he was going down out of the trees and onto the greying prairie where the first streaks of a new day were slitting their way across the soft underbelly of the night.

He went by way of his soddy. There he stopped long enough to clean up, shave and change his clothing. The musty, lonely smell of the cabin drove him to finish what he had to do as fast as he could and ride down the land toward Malta with fresher smells of a new day in his face.

By the time he rode into the northern approaches of the town the place was a beehive of speculation and activity. News of the fight had come back with the men he had sent for the buggy and the doctor. He saw men eyeing him with wondering interest. His face was set in a harsh and melancholy expression. None approached him although, when he swung down before the sheriff's office and tied up, several of the more curious, and least inhibited, walked toward him. He turned and gazed steadily at the nearest man, then brushing past he pushed open the office door, stepped through it and closed it quietly behind himself.

A stout, clear-eyed grey-headed woman was sitting behind Marlow's table. She glanced up at him, waiting. They both knew who the other was and Mrs. Marlow said nothing because there was nothing she need say. Jack crossed the room in stony silence, pulled a chair away from the wall and dropped down on it heavily. Pushing his hat back he studied the woman's face for a moment before he spoke. Her mouth was pulled inward with worry and anxiety but her eyes were fearless and steady. He liked that.

"Amos stopped one in the hip, but it isn't bad. Through the meat, ma'm, is all. He'll be down for a while, but that's about all." She nodded, still waiting. "There's a dead one."

"I heard it was Old Man Burrows; was it?"

"Yes. The young one — his son, Mark — got creased alongside the head. It looks pretty messy but I couldn't find any busted skull and I poked for it. I reckon he'll come out of it, too."

"Any others?"

"No'm." He watched her relax and lean back in the chair. She seemed to lose some of the starch that had held her upright. After a moment she began speaking. The words were clipped, to the point and frank. "Amos told me about you. So did the girl. I had another talk with her a little while ago. I thought she ought to know — be told by someone besides Amos — I know how blunt he is at times like this."

"Ma'm," Jack interrupted wearily, slowly, never taking his eyes from her face. "I know what she told you. I don't feel like tryin' to justify what I've done, but I'll tell you right now I *didn't* make a fool of her, so I'd be able to catch her father and brother."

"I didn't believe you did, Jack," Mrs. Marlow said quietly. "I don't believe any real man would do that. I told her that. She has an awful lot of pain inside her and you can't blame her for what she thinks and the way she feels. In her place I'd probably feel the same way, and you would, too."

"Yes'm, I guess that's right."

"It's a good sign, I think, that she's finally decided to talk at all. If she gets it out of her system I think there's hope for you two."

"Us two?" he said softly. "How do you mean, ma'm?"

"You're in love with her, aren't you?"

"Yes."

"She's in love with you, too, Mister Fulton, I can tell you that with no doubt at all in my mind about it. Hate and love are very close. She hates you now with a terrible hatred. I don't think she realizes it herself, but she loves you with just as terrible a love. You're a man, so I don't expect you to understand what I'm saying. All I'd like you to do is leave her alone for a little while. Let me —"

"That's what I rode on ahead for, ma'm. I didn't want Amos or anyone else to tell her about her paw and her brother. I wanted to tell her myself."

"Why?"

Jack looked past the older woman with a sadness that was deep. "I thought it'd be better for two reasons. She already hates me worse'n a rattler. If she blames me for *all* her grief it'll keep her from hating the others — Amos, for instance — and she can't hate me worse, no matter what I tell her. The other reason was because I wanted to tell her exactly how everything happened, not leave that for her to hear third hand. There's another thing, too. She doesn't know what her paw and brother were up to. I found that out from Mark. I want to tell it all to her straight."

"There's plenty of time for that, Jack," Mrs. Marlow said. "I think you're trying to be too honest. I mean, you handle men like that, but not women. Let her know about her father and brother's fight, then leave her alone. When she's over that shock a little, wait for her to come around and ask. By then she'll be rational enough to understand the rest of it."

He turned it over in his mind dully. The silence in the office lasted a long time. The sheriff's wife watched his face. He had to dredge up a defensive blankness to hide his anguish. He hid it so well that when the possemen came into the office with Amos on their arms, none of them saw anything but the tall, gaunt frame of Jack Fulton stretched out in his chair with a very tired, listless look on his face.

The sheriff was made comfortable on two chairs and an angry-eyed doctor stood stiffly glowering down at him. Amos smiled ruggedly at his wife, winked very sombrely, then gave Jack the same grin. "Why'd you hurry off, Jack? Don't answer. I know." He turned to a greying man beside him. "Lewt, get the names of every man that rode with us and make me up a pay-sheet for 'em, will you?" The other nodded in silence and Amos turned to a roomful of tired, heavily-armed riders. "Thanks, boys. I'll see that you get your money. We won't need you any more."

The possemen shuffled outside into the warming day and Amos motioned for the doctor to close the door behind them. He shifted a little on his two chairs, winced, swore softly and looked at Jack again. "Son, I've got to ask you to do me a favour. You're still on the payroll, anyway."

"What?"

"Someone's got to take a crew back up there and dig the gold out of those cattle."

Jack said nothing. He let his glance slide off the sheriff's face. Mrs. Marlow spoke in her incise, straightforward way. "That's exactly what you need, Jack. Not only you, either. Go up there and do that. It'll take a little time. When you're finished come back and see me. Will you?"

He got up slowly and nodded at the sheriff's wife. "Yes'm. I'll do it, but because Amos can't — not because I think you're going to make any headway with what you've got in mind."

Mrs. Marlow accepted the challenge with a brusque nod and Amos looked up at his deputy sheriff. "They'll be scattered all over kingdom come, Jack. You know how many's there, don't you?"

"Yeh."

"Fine. Get some breakfast and come back here. By then I'll have Dutch and Lewt and a couple more boys lined up to help you. Is that all right?"

"Yeh."

The work took two days — two days of gruelling, constant labour.

The second day they finished, but Jack vetoed returning until the following day. They bedded down and slept with a fortune in blood-stained, coarse-grain gold beside them, and Jack had the relief he had known he'd find, in a black, selfless sleep so deep and solid he didn't awaken until the sun was making yellow spots under his eyelids and the others were already up and saddling. He was still as silent as a tomb but the deputies had become accustomed to it, adopting a kind of blunt directness that minimised words, themselves.

They beat the worst part of the heat to Malta, where the gold was laid before the two perspiring men from the Territorial Capitol and Jack was halfway back through the door when one of the strangers stopped him with a quick frown and an upheld hand. "Just a minute there. You're Jack Fulton, aren't you?"

"I am."

"There are some things we'd like to talk over with you."

Jack's brooding, hooded glance showed

disdain and impatience. "Hasn't Amos told you all the details?"

"Yes, but there's —"

"Get the rest of it from him." He went out and left an awkward silence behind him. "Doesn't talk much," one of the deputies said apologetically, fingering his tobacco sack and looking a little embarrassed. Amos made a trifling wave with one hand.

"Leave him be. He's lost more'n a brother in this business. Whatever you want to know further, ask me. In a couple months I'll sit down and get him to write out his report of it, but right now don't push him around any."

"Well," the red-faced man from the Capitol said, "that's about all we wanted anyway, sheriff. That and the gold, here."

Amos smiled a little, wanly. "For us it's all over; for Jack Fulton only the shooting's over."

Jack met the doctor in his office without any sense or awareness of the victory he had achieved. He stood tall and melancholy, looking into the medical man's face. "Mark come around yet?"

"Yes. Come on, I'll let you see him."

Mark's head was swathed in a balloon-like bandage. His eyes stared dryly up at Jack from the pale, sunken setting of his face.

Jack didn't move toward the chair beside the bed until the doctor left them alone, then he seated himself with a slumped posture, looking straight into the younger man's face. "You know about Abe?"

"And Suzanne?"

"What about her, you dirty —"

"Hold it! Sheriff Marlow's wife's doing everything she can to bring her around, Mark. Don't blame me or anyone else for what she's been through. There's only two people on earth responsible, and you know it."

The wounded man's sullenness seemed, strangely, to lift a little. "It's all over," he said in a quiet, abstract way.

"You ought to be glad, Mark. You're not an outlaw. You're not built that way. Do you know who I am? My name, I mean?"

"Yeah, the sawbones told me." There was no anger, just weariness and resignation in the voice. "Fulton, the feller the old man wanted killed."

"You know your brother Colt got what was coming to him. I wouldn't have downed him, Mark, if I'd known the rest of this was like it was."

"What're you talkin' about?"

"Your sister."

Mark's gaze went slowly to Jack's face

with wonder and dawning surprise in it. "You — did you know Suzanne before?"

"Yeah. Listen, Mark. Your paw drygulched my brother. I came out here to settle up for that and got your brother in the bargain. The rest of it's pretty simple. You fellers didn't know me by sight. That's what saved my hide south of the border. I tried to get you to come out of the cabin the night of the fight because I knew you didn't have too much heart in the smuggling business. I still don't think you're an outlaw, inside of you, where it counts." He straightened up on the chair before he went on. Mark's glance was steady on his face.

"I came in here today to tell you I figure to do everything I can do, to get you out of trouble. Maybe you'll have to go to Yuma for year or two — I don't know. I'll fight that too, Mark. All I want in return is your word of honour you won't go outside the law again."

"What's your interest, now, Fulton?"

"Suzanne."

"Oh." Mark stared at him. "I ought to hate your guts," he said.

Jack stood up, slouched and hip-shot. "No, we're even. I didn't down Abe at the fight. In fact I didn't try to get either one of you. I hoped it might end like this and I

257

didn't want it any other way. Abe killed my brother. I killed Colt. Your smuggling ring's smashed and — it's all over, Mark. All I want now is for you to promise me, for your own sake and Suzanne's, you'll stay inside the law. That, and maybe your hand, if you'll give it."

Mark's stoniness lasted until Jack thought he wasn't going to speak. But he did. "I've done some thinkin' too, Fulton." He stuck out his hand. "Here."

They shook and Jack had a little trouble with the tightness of his throat. "I'll come back later, Mark, and let you know what your chances are. All right?"

"Fair enough," Mark said evenly. He didn't bid Jack good-bye and Jack didn't say it either when he left the room. The doctor was waiting for him with a questioning look.

"Mister Fulton —"

"Keep it, Doc. I'll be back later."

He went around to Sheriff Marlow's house and rapped gently on the door. Mrs. Marlow met him with a gesture to enter. He doffed his hat and went into the parlour.

"How is she, ma'm?" His answer was a silent little bob of Mrs. Marlow's head past him. He turned with a sinking feeling, for he had thought Suzanne was still in jail over at Amos' office. She was sitting on a leather sofa behind him, looking up at him with a blank, unnerving stare.

He felt his heart lurch and the rust-coloured blood stain his face and there wasn't a thing he could think of to say. It was one of those thoroughly demoralising, terrible moments every man experiences some time in his life.

Mrs. Marlow watched them both with her lips pulled back against her teeth, scarcely breathing. Jack had a wretched ten seconds, then he turned away with a strangling feeling, holding his hat like it was his sole link with life.

"I'll go," he said, and moved awkwardly toward the door again.

"Just a minute, Jack," Mrs. Marlow said. "Have you seen Mark?"

"Yes, just left him, why?"

"Suzanne and I were up there last night talking to him. I told the doctor to tell you she was here, now."

"Oh." He remembered the doctor trying to tell hint something. "I didn't wait," he said vaguely.

"Mark talked to her a long time. He isn't as vengeance minded as I thought he might be."

Jack drew in a deep breath, turned his head just enough to see Suzanne's face, and let the words come out slowly. "Suzanne, I told Mark I'd do everything I can for him. I'm going to see the judge now. I'll tell Mark everything I find out. He can tell you."

The girl's rich brown eyes hadn't left his face since he'd turned and faced her. She spoke so low he hardly heard her. "All right," she said. "Thank you." Her lips trembled, but nothing more came.

Mrs. Marlow took his arm and firmly piloted him outside the door and down the walk before she let go and smiled up at him. "There's your answer, Jack," she said with a tight lilt to her voice.

"It didn't sound like much to me," he said glumly.

Exasperation showed briefly in Mrs. Marlow's face. "Don't expect miracles, young man. They just don't happen at a time like this. Be patient, son; be patient and pray. That's what Amos and I've been doing, and you'd be surprised at what'll come of it. She's going to come around all right. I *know* she is. I thought so all along but after this, I'm surer than ever. Now, go see the judge and don't come back until day after tomorrow. By then I'll have taken her to see her brother again. It isn't just you that's been a terrible shock to her. It's what her menfolk were doing, too. Now go get shaved and cleaned up and eat heartily. You've lost a lot of weight from the looks of you. Eat a lot, get some rest — and come back day after tomorrow and I'll promise you a surprise."

He looked hopefully at her and felt his spirits come up a little. "Do you think it'll be all right — for sure, ma'm?"

"I'll promise you it will. Now go on."

He went. There was a little of the old, confident swing to his long stride as he headed back up-town.